This book should be returned to any branch of the
Lancashire County Library on or before the date shown

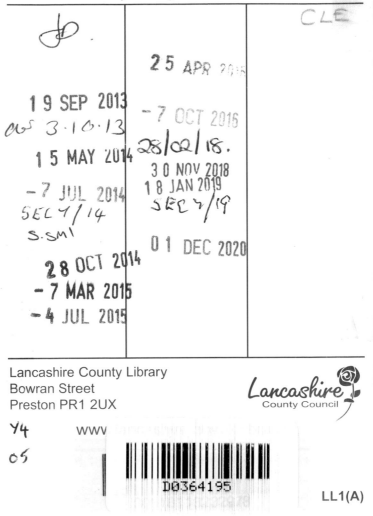

Lancashire County Library
Bowran Street
Preston PR1 2UX

Lancashire
County Council

Y4
05

www

LL1(A)

Dear Reader

A turquoise ocean, palm-fringed beaches, and lazy days spent sipping cocktails from a sunlit veranda... What better way to try to mend a broken heart and lay plans for the future?

That's what I had in mind when I set out to write Alyssa and Connor's story. An exotic paradise island seemed to me to be the very best setting for their romance. Anything can happen. Dreams can come true...eventually.

Even paradise can suffer storm clouds now and again, though, and that's exactly what happens to Alyssa's attempts to restore her soul. Of course she needs a very special person to make her dreams come true...

Enjoy!

Joanna

When **Joanna Neil** discovered Mills & Boon®, her lifelong addiction to reading crystallised into an exciting new career writing Medical Romance™. Her characters are probably the outcome of her varied lifestyle, which includes working as a clerk, typist, nurse and infant teacher. She enjoys dressmaking and cooking at her Leicestershire home. Her family includes a husband, son and daughter, an exuberant yellow Labrador and two slightly crazed cockatiels. She currently works with a team of tutors at her local education centre to provide creative writing workshops for people interested in exploring their own writing ambitions.

HIS BRIDE IN PARADISE

BY
JOANNA NEIL

First published in Great Britain 2012
by Mills & Boon, an imprint of Harlequin (UK) Limited.
Large Print edition 2013
Harlequin (UK) Limited, Eton House,
18-24 Paradise Road, Richmond, Surrey TW9 1SR

© Joanna Neil 2012

ISBN: 978 0 263 23114 4   11823297

Harlequin (UK) policy is to use papers that are
natural, renewable and recyclable products and made
from wood grown in sustainable forests. The logging
and manufacturing process conform to the legal
environmental regulations of the country of origin.

Printed and bound in Great Britain
by CPI Antony Rowe, Chippenham, Wiltshire

Recent titles by Joanna Neil:

TAMED BY HER BROODING BOSS
DR RIGHT ALL ALONG
DR LANGLEY: PROTECTOR OR PLAYBOY?
A COTSWOLD CHRISTMAS BRIDE
THE TAMING OF DR ALEX DRAYCOTT
BECOMING DR BELLINI'S BRIDE

**These books are also available in eBook format
from www.millsandboon.co.uk**

CHAPTER ONE

'I CAN'T believe my luck,' Alyssa said excitedly, cradling the phone close to her ear. 'The house is magnificent, Carys, and it's right next to the ocean.'

'Mmm…that's exactly how I imagined it,' her cousin answered. 'So you managed to find the place all right? How's it all going for you?' On the other end of the line, Carys's voice held a note of eager anticipation.

Alyssa smiled at her enthusiastic tone. Carys lived on the mainland in Florida, some sixty or seventy miles away from here, and she was keen to know everything that was going on.

'Oh, it was easy enough,' Alyssa said. 'The taxi driver dropped me off. Apparently everyone around here knows the Blakeley property.' She adjusted the fluffy bath towel around her damp body. She'd not long come from the shower and had been sitting for a few minutes by the dressing table, blowdrying her long hair so that the mass of chestnut-coloured curls gleamed softly in the lamplight. 'I'm doing just fine,' she added. 'It's lovely here. You wouldn't believe how beautiful it is.'

She left the dresser and went to settle down on the luxurious softness of the large divan bed, stretching out her long, slender limbs. 'I only arrived here a couple of hours ago, so I haven't really had time to look around, but the house is perfect. There are double glass doors everywhere, even in the bedrooms, and when you step out onto the deck you look out over the Atlantic Ocean. It's fantastic, Carys…it's so incredibly blue.'

A faint breeze wafted in through the open veranda doors, and glancing there from across the room Alyssa could see the branches of the palm trees swaying gently against the skyline of the setting sun. Birds called to one another, sleepy in the warm evening air. 'I'm sitting here now, and I can hear the waves breaking on the shore.'

'It sounds heavenly.'

'Mmm, it is.' Alyssa couldn't believe her change in fortune. Within a few weeks she'd gone from enduring a bleak, desperately unhappy situation back in the UK to finding herself in this idyllic haven on a sand-fringed island in the Bahamas. 'I keep thinking that any minute now someone will come along and pinch me and tell me it's all a dream.'

Carys chuckled. 'No, I think it's really happening. Is Ross there with you? I know he was keen to help you get settled in.'

'No. He rang to tell me he'd be along a little later. He had a meeting with the director so that they could iron out a few things before filming starts tomorrow.'

Alyssa stopped to listen for a moment as a faint creaking sound caught her attention, like a footfall on the steps leading to the deck. Was someone walking around outside? Could it be that there was a change of plan and Ross was coming home earlier than expected? Then one of the voile curtains fluttered on a light current of air, distracting her, and she shook her head. Ross had stressed the importance of the meeting. It must have been the door that was creaking, that would be it.

'Well, he'll make sure that everything goes smoothly for you, I'm sure,' Carys murmured. 'You can put all your troubles behind you now, and forget about your awful ex. I've known Ross for ages, and he has a heart of gold. He'll take good care of you. I know he was besotted with you from the moment he set eyes on you.'

Alyssa sat up against the pillows. 'Oh, no… surely that can't be true… At least, I hope it isn't.' Ross knew how she felt. She'd come here to get away from all the mess that relationships involved, clutching at the chance Ross had given her to make her escape. This was her sanctuary.

Her work back in the UK had proved to be a stumbling block, too, and she'd reluctantly decided to put what had once been a promising medical career temporarily on hold. At least, she hoped it was only a relatively short-term move. In the end, things had proved too much for her, and she'd had to accept that she needed to take time out to recover from the burnout that had crept up on her and caught her unawares.

Somehow, she had to try to get herself back together again and she was pinning her hopes on the healing qualities of these next few months. As to the rest…

'I've finished with romance,' she said, her tone quiet and restrained. 'I'm done with all that.'

'So you say.' Carys laughed. 'Anyway, your ex is finally out of the picture, so with a bit of luck you can relax now and look forward to a few months of sheer luxury and self-indulgence.'

'Well, of course,' Alyssa answered, tongue in cheek. 'How could I not enjoy all this? I've got it made, haven't I? Nothing much to do but enjoy the sunshine and surf and thank my lucky stars. I'll take money and all these rich trappings over love any time. Who wouldn't?'

'Sure you will,' Carys murmured drily. She knew full well that Alyssa was joking. 'Look,

I have to go. I'll call you again. You take care. Love you.'

'And you.'

Alyssa cut the call and put down the phone, listening once more as the creaking grew louder. *Was* someone or something out there? It couldn't be Ross, surely? He'd said he would be delayed for at least an hour. Frowning, she went over to the doors and stepped out onto the deck.

A white ibis caught her attention in the distance, wandering along the shoreline, dipping his long red bill into the shallows in search of any tasty morsels that might have been washed up by the sea. She watched him for a moment or two.

'We see those birds quite often around here,' a male voice said, catching her completely unawares. The deep, resonant tones smoothed over her, making her swivel around in startled surprise.

The man moved from the shelter of the open sitting-room door and came to stand just a couple of feet away from her. He leaned negligently against the rail, making himself completely at home.

'Who—who are you…? What are you doing here?' She stared at him, shocked, wide-eyed, a little afraid and uncertain as to what to do. She was completely alone out here. He was at least six feet tall, long limbed, broad shouldered, definitely a force to be reckoned with.

She quickly thought through her options. The neighbours were too distant to hear if she were to shout out, and for an instant she floundered, before self-preservation took hold. Maybe he *was* a neighbour, and she was simply jumping to conclusions. Just because he was standing on Ross's veranda, it didn't have to mean he was some kind of would-be felon…did it?

'I was originally planning on helping myself to a cool drink and something to eat,' he answered with a faint shrug. 'I thought the place was empty, but then I heard a woman's voice and thought maybe I'd better find out who was here.'

His glance travelled over her, gliding along the creamy slope of her bare shoulders, moving down across the brief white towel that clung to her curves and coming to linger for a while on the golden expanse of her shapely legs. His gaze shifted downwards. Her feet were bare, her toenails painted a delicate shade of pink, and there were tiny gemstones embedded in the pearly nail varnish. A faint smile touched his mouth. 'I certainly hadn't expected to find anyone quite so lovely here to greet me.'

Alyssa felt warm colour invade her cheeks and her fingers tightened on the towel, clutching it to her breasts. He seemed to be quite at ease here, yet he still hadn't explained who he was.

'Well, whoever you are, you shouldn't be here,' she said. What kind of person would have the gall to calmly walk in and help himself to a drink? Ross had insisted she would have the place to herself. Her green eyes flashed a warning. 'You'd better go before I call the police.'

Belatedly, she remembered that she'd left her phone on the bedside table. Could she sidle back into the room and dial the number without alert-

ing him to her actions? Hardly. Still, a bit of bravado wouldn't come amiss, would it?

He'd made no attempt to move. 'I can't think
why you're still standing there,' she said in a terse
voice. 'I meant what I said.'

'Yes, I realise that… I just don't think it's a
very good idea.'

'Of course you don't. You wouldn't, would you?
Even so…' She took a couple of steps backwards
into the bedroom, not taking her eyes off him for
a second. The smooth, Italian-tiled floor was cool
beneath her feet, soothing to her ragged nerves.
Her heart was pounding, her pulse thumping out
an erratic beat.

He didn't look the least bit put out. He was
dressed in cool, expensive-looking chinos and
a loose cotton shirt. His hair was dark, the perfect styling framing an angular face, but it was
his eyes that held her most of all… They were
narrowed on her now, grey, like the sea on a
stormy night, and compelling, a hint of something unknown glimmering in their depths as
he studied her.

Slowly, he pushed himself away from the rail and began to move towards her, and her insides lurched in fearful acknowledgement. Instinctively, she recognised that this was a man who knew what he wanted and who was used to getting his own way. He wasn't going anywhere, and it certainly didn't look as though he intended to heed her warning.

She felt behind her for the mobile phone on the bedside table.

'As I said, I really wouldn't advise you do that,' he murmured, his gaze following her actions. 'You might find yourself having to explain to them what exactly you're doing in my house.'

Her jaw dropped a fraction. '*Your* house?' She frowned, then shot him a steely glance. 'No…no, that can't be right. You're the intruder, not me. I'll tell them so.'

There was a glint in his dark eyes. 'Okay, let's get this straight—I'm Connor Blakeley, and this has actually been my home for a number of years. My brother lives here too, from time to time, but it's a fact that it's my name on the deeds of the property.' He studied her. 'So, would you like to tell me who you are and what you're doing here?' His mouth moved in a wry smile. 'Or perhaps I can hazard a guess. This is bound to be something to do with Ross. You must be his latest girlfriend.'

She stiffened. He made it sound as though there had been a stream of them. Deciding to ignore his comment, she shook her head so that her bright curls tumbled about her shoulders. This man had to be an imposter, surely? Doubts were beginning to creep in, but she said cautiously, 'Connor's away for the next six months. Ross told me so. His brother's in Florida, helping to organise a new medical emergency unit over there.'

He nodded briefly. 'That was true. Unfortunately an urgent situation occurred right here in the Bahamas, and I was asked to come back and take over the accident and emergency department at the hospital. So I'll be working here and at the same time I'll be keeping an eye on the Florida unit from a distance.'

Her indrawn breath was sharp and audible.

What he said sounded plausible enough. Could it be that she'd made a mistake in doubting him? He did look a bit like Ross, now she came to think of it.

Carefully, she replaced the phone on the table and straightened up. Now what was she to do? Her cheeks burned with colour. How could she have ended up in such a humiliating situation? Hadn't she put up with enough of those back in England? This was meant to have been a fresh start, and now it looked as though her expectations of spending a relaxed, trouble-free few months out here were being rapidly consigned to the rubbish bin.

She lifted her chin, determined to pull herself together. It was a setback, that was all. Somehow she would sort this out and find herself another place to stay. She just had to hope that the cost wouldn't be way beyond her means. It had only been Ross's conviction that she could stay in this house rent-free that had persuaded her she could afford to come out here in the first place.

'I'm really sorry,' she said. 'I'd no idea… I

wasn't expecting anyone else to be here tonight.'
She hesitated, drawing in a calming breath. 'I'm
Alyssa Morgan. Your brother invited me to stay
here.'

'Was he planning on staying here with you?'

She frowned. 'Not with me, exactly. He said
he would take the upper-floor accommodation,
and I could have the downstairs apartment.' She
looked across the room to where her suitcases
stood against the louvred doors of the wardrobe.
She hadn't even had time to unpack. 'But, of
course, it's all changed now. I'll get my things
together and find somewhere else to stay.'

'At this time of the evening?' He raised a dark
brow. 'Even supposing you could find anywhere
at such short notice, I couldn't let you do that.
I've a feeling that an attractive young woman
alone in the city would be far too great a tempta-
tion for some of our, shall we say, less civilised,
male citizens?'

She straightened her shoulders. 'I can take care
of myself.'

His glance moved over her. 'Really?'

His obvious disbelief stung. She felt his dark gaze linger on her slender curves, and she hugged the towel to herself in a defensive gesture. With so much pale golden skin on display she felt she was at a distinct disadvantage. 'Anyway, I should get dressed,' she said, with as much dignity as she could muster. 'If you wouldn't mind…?'

He nodded. 'Of course.' He started to walk across the room but stopped by the door to look back and say, 'You seem a bit flushed. Perhaps I could get you an iced drink and maybe something to eat? Or have you already had supper?'

Her eyes widened. She wasn't expecting such generosity, given the circumstances, and it only made her feel worse, after the way she'd spoken to him. 'No…um…I haven't had time… I only arrived here a short time ago, and I was feeling hot and dusty after the flight and so on, so I decided to have a shower before I did anything else. Ross and I were going to have supper when…' She broke off, then added, 'He had to go to a meeting.'

'Hmm.' Connor was frowning as he looked

at the suitcases. 'I take it from your accent that you're English. Is that right? Did you and Ross meet over in the UK? I know he was over there scouting for talent for his latest film project.'

'Yes, we did.' Connor was American-English, she knew, as his father had been born in the United States and his mother was from London. 'We…uh…have a mutual friend over in Florida… my cousin, Carys…and she suggested he look me up.'

'Oh, yes. I know Carys.' He made a faint smile as he studied her. 'I expect Ross was glad he took the time to follow up on that.' He started to turn back towards the door. 'Well, maybe I'll make a start on preparing some food and then Ross can join us when he gets here.'

'I… Yes, that would be good. Thank you.' Her head was reeling. How on earth would Ross react on finding that his brother was here? One way or another, he was in for something of a shock.

Connor left the room and Alyssa pulled in a deep breath. It wasn't the best way for her to have met Connor, was it? She'd heard quite a bit about him from Ross, and her overall impression was that Ross was a little in awe of his older brother. Now that she'd met him, she could certainly understand why. There was that quality about him, something that suggested he would always be in complete control of any situation, that nothing would faze him. Everything about him underlined that. He was supple and lithe, his body honed with latent energy, and a calm, inherent sense of authority oozed from every pore.

She dressed quickly, choosing a pale blue cotton dress with narrow straps, cool enough for the warmth of the evening. It wasn't much in the way of a defence, but at least being fully dressed made her feel more in command of herself.

A few minutes later she walked into the kitchen and found Connor busy at the table, adding tomato paste and grated cheese to a large pizza base. He looked up as she entered the room. 'You look fresh and cool,' he murmured. 'That colour suits you.'

'Thank you.'

'Sit down,' he said, waving her to a chair by

the pale oak table. 'Would you like mushrooms with this? And peppers?'

'Yes, please.' She nodded, watching as he deftly cut and sliced mushrooms and then sprinkled them over the cheese.

She glanced around. From here, by the deep, broad window, she could look out over the ocean, and closer to home there was what seemed to be a small kitchen garden just beyond the veranda. The light outside was fading now, but solar lamps sent a golden glow over a variety of vegetables and a small grove of trees laden with plump, ripe oranges.

She turned her attention back to the kitchen. 'You have a beautiful home,' she said. The kitchen was full of state-of-the-art equipment, along with a tiled island bar and glass shelving that housed colourful ceramics and delicately sculpted vases.

'Thanks.' He smiled. 'I must admit I'm pleased with it. When I moved here I wanted a house where I would be able to relax and shrug off the cares of the day, and this seemed to be the perfect place in an idyllic setting…a small piece of paradise, if you like. I sit out on the deck of an evening and watch the waves breaking on the shore. It's very relaxing, especially if you like to watch wildlife, as I do. You sometimes see herons and egrets around here, and there might even be a golden plover that appears from time to time.'

'It sounds idyllic.'

'It is.' He slid the pizza into the hot oven and came over to the table, picking up a jug of iced juice. 'Would you like a drink? I can get you something stronger if you prefer.'

'Thanks…orange juice will be fine.' She made a face. 'I'm not used to this heat. I seem to have been thirsty ever since I arrived here.'

His mouth curved. 'You get used to it after a while. I have air-conditioning, but sometimes I prefer to throw open all the doors and windows and let the sea air in.'

'Yes, I can understand that. I think I would, too.' She sipped the cold juice, pausing to rest the glass momentarily against her throat to cool her heated skin. His glance followed her movements, but his eyes were dark and unreadable.

'So, you and Ross must be working together on his new film, I suppose?' he commented. He poured himself a glass of juice and took a long swallow, looking at her over the rim. 'He and I haven't talked much about the casting, but I can see why he must have wanted to bring you over here. I imagine you're very photogenic. And I guess you must have auditioned well.'

'Um…that's not exactly what happened,' she murmured. She frowned. He obviously had the wrong idea, if he was assuming she was an actress. 'I'm really not expecting to have anything to do with the filming as such.'

'Ah…that's interesting.' He shot her an assessing glance. 'Still, he must think a lot of you, to have brought you over here and set you up in the family home. After all, you can't have known each other very long.'

Alyssa put down her glass, her mouth firming into a straight line. 'Um…I don't know, but…I think you must have the wrong idea. I get the impression that you've put two and two together and made five.'

'Have I?' His mouth tilted in disbelief. 'I may have some of the facts wrong, but in essence I know my brother pretty well, and this wouldn't be the first time he's fallen for a young woman and gone out of his way to throw the world at her feet.' There was a gleam in his eyes. 'Unfortunately for him, this time he wasn't expecting me to turn up out of the blue. I can see how that might make things a bit difficult.'

She stood up. 'You know, on second thoughts, I don't think this arrangement is going to work out after all. I think I'll go with my original plan and find somewhere else to stay.'

She started to move away from the table, but he caught hold of her, his fingers curving around her bare arm. 'Please don't do that, Alyssa, it's really not a good idea.'

'Maybe so, but that's my worry, not yours.'

She tried to pull away from him, but he simply drew her closer to him, so that her soft curves brushed against his long body. 'I'm afraid it's very much my problem,' he said, 'since my brother has seen fit to install you under my roof.'

'You make me sound as though I'm a package to be parcelled up by your brother and shipped wherever the fancy takes him,' she said in a terse voice. 'That's not only insulting, it's downright chauvinistic. Where have you been living these last thirty or so years? It's obvious to me that your mind-set is stuck somewhere in the last century.'

He laughed. It wasn't what she was expecting, and anger and frustration rose up in her like mercury shooting up a gauge on a blazing hot day. 'You'd better let me go right now,' she said, 'or I swear you won't like the consequences.' When he didn't release her, she started to bring her knee up, ready to deliver a crippling blow, and he swiftly turned her round so that his arms encased her from behind. Frustratingly, she was locked into his embrace, her spine resting against his taut, masculine frame.

'Of course I'll let you go,' he murmured, 'if you promise me that you won't try to leave before morning. I apologise if I've been jumping to conclusions. I've been assuming that Ross is behaving in his usual hedonistic manner, but I have to admit you're very different from what I might have expected. You're not at all like his usual choice of women.'

'Is that so?' She was rigid in his arms, still seething with indignation.

'I didn't mean to offend you,' he said. 'Honestly. I'm trying to explain. Look at it from my point of view. I had no idea that he was bringing anyone home. He usually tells me. So why didn't he do that if everything was open and above board? For all he knew, I might have arranged for a friend to stay here while I was away. That's why we always tell each other about our plans.'

'Perhaps he acted on impulse and meant to tell you later.' Her body relaxed a fraction.

'Yes, I suppose that could be it.' He nodded, and his cheek lightly brushed hers. His hold on her eased a little, and it seemed to Alyssa's heightened senses that it became much more like a caress. She felt his warm breath fall softly on the back of her neck, and his arm brushed the rounded swell of her breast as he held her to him.

It was unintentional, she was sure, but the heated contact ricocheted through her body, bringing with it a shocking, bone-melting response. She closed her eyes, breathing deeply. How could she be reacting this way? She didn't even know him. It was unthinkable.

Clearly there was something wrong with her. Jet-lag, probably. She needed to break free from him, but the warmth of those encircling arms and the gentleness of that embrace had taken her completely by surprise. It seemed like such a long time since anyone had held her in such an intimate way and, worryingly, she was discovering that she liked it.

'I'll find somewhere else to stay first thing in the morning,' she said.

Slowly, almost reluctantly, he released her. 'You don't need to do that. You're Ross's guest, and therefore mine, too. I wouldn't dream of having you go elsewhere. Please stay. I'd like you to stay.'

'I'll think about it.' She dithered for a moment. She wanted to walk out of the room, but as she stood there, undecided, she glanced towards the oven, conscious of the appetising smell of melting cheese and sizzling herbs and tomato permeating the air. She hadn't realised until now how hungry she was...her last meal had been virtually a snack on the plane journey over here.

He looked at her, his head tilted on one side, a faint smile playing around his mouth. 'You're hungry,' he said. 'It's no wonder you're feeling a little fractious. Sit down and we'll eat. Things always seem better on a full stomach.'

Annoyed by her own weakness, she did as he suggested and went back to the chair. Maybe he was right, and circumstances had combined to throw her off balance. A long plane journey, a change of surroundings and the appearance of the proverbial tall, dark stranger had certainly knocked her for six. Her heart was racing as though she'd run a marathon, and the world seemed to be spinning around her ever so slightly. She felt decidedly odd.

There was a noise from across the room and

they both turned as the kitchen door opened and Ross came in.

'What on earth…? Connor, what are you doing here? Aren't you supposed to be in Florida?' He was tall, like his brother, with dark hair and the same angular jaw, but Ross had more homely, lived-in features, and generally there was a happy-go-lucky, almost boyish air about him. 'You said you'd be away for several months.'

'I did, but there was a change of plan. It turns out I'm going to be working here, on the island, for the most part.'

'So you'll be staying here.' It was a matter-of-fact statement. Then Ross added, 'I've arranged for Alyssa to have the ground-floor apartment. I'd no idea you would be coming back so soon.'

Connor nodded. 'Yes, she told me. That's okay. That arrangement can still stand. It just means that you'll have to stay at your place near the film studio. That won't be a problem for you, will it?'

Ross's grey-blue eyes narrowed. 'I guess not.' He looked at his brother as though he suspected him of some devious ploy.

'Good. So now that's all sorted, perhaps we can sit down together and enjoy a meal.'

Connor took the pizza from the oven, and Alyssa said quietly, 'Is there anything I can do to help? I could set the table for you, if you like.'

'Thanks. That would be great. There's a bowl of salad in the fridge. You could put that out, too, if you would.'

'Okay.'

They worked together, while Ross went to freshen up. 'So, if you're not involved with the filming, what will you be doing all day while Ross is at work?' Connor asked. 'Is this meant to be a holiday for you, or a sightseeing trip, or something like that?'

Alyssa smiled. 'It's nothing like that. I'm going to be working as a medic on the film set. Apparently, the company Ross usually calls on to provide that service is tied up with other projects right now, so when he found out that I was looking for work, he asked me if I'd like to take it on.'

Connor's dark brows lifted. 'You're a nurse?'

She shook her head. 'I'm a doctor. I've worked

in the same line as you, accident and emergency, so I should be able to deal with any problems that arise if stunts go wrong, and so on.' She smiled. 'Though, hopefully, that won't happen. Mostly, it'll be a case of handing out headache and sunburn medication, I expect.'

'So now you've managed to surprise me all over again.' Connor stared at her for a moment or two, before starting to slice the pizza into triangular wedges. 'Now I understand what you meant when you told your friend that there would be nothing much to do but enjoy the sunshine and the surf and thank your lucky stars.'

She frowned, sending him a fleeting glance. 'You heard me talking to Carys on the phone?'

He nodded. 'I didn't know it was Carys, but I heard some of the conversation you were having. I came out onto the deck and I couldn't help but hear what you were saying.' He paused as he checked the filter on the coffee pot.

'The only part that bothered me was when you added that you'd take money and all the trappings over love any time.' His gaze meshed with hers. 'I don't know what your plans are, but perhaps I should warn you to tread carefully there. I wouldn't want to see my brother hurt. He has his faults, but he's family and I care about him very much.'

Once again this evening she felt hot colour rise in her cheeks. No wonder he'd been so edgy with her from the beginning. He'd heard what she said and had drawn his own conclusions.

'It was just a joke,' she said. 'The sort of throwaway remark we all make from time to time. It didn't mean anything.'

'Maybe so.' He acknowledged that with a wry smile, but she noticed the warmth didn't reach his dark eyes. 'But the warning stands... I've always looked out for my brother, and I see no reason to stop doing that.'

'Even though he's a grown man who owns a successful film company? Don't you trust him to make his own decisions?'

'Of course I do...to a certain extent. But Ross is a fool where women are concerned. He's made a few mistakes over the years that have cost him dearly. I don't want to see that happen again.'

'And I'm obviously the scarlet woman whose talons cut deep?' She sent him a scornful look.

'You've come all the way from the UK to be with him.' His mouth twisted. 'I don't blame you for that. Who would turn down the chance of living a life of luxury on this beautiful island? But I'm inclined to be cautious all the same.'

Clearly he wasn't going to believe she was on the level. Alyssa opened her mouth to make an answering retort, but Ross came back into the kitchen just then, and she concentrated instead on carefully laying out the cutlery on the table.

'I'm starving,' Ross said, eyeing the food with a ravenous eye. 'This looks good.'

She smiled at him, handing him a plate, and took her seat at the table. She didn't need to say anything more to Connor. They simply looked at one another, and that glance spoke volumes. They both knew exactly where they stood. He didn't trust her an inch and for her part she was ultra-wary of him. The battle lines were drawn.

CHAPTER TWO

'ARE we all clear for this shot?' Ross was talking to the cameraman, making sure that every detail was covered. They were standing just a few yards away from Alyssa, and she could hear every word that was being said. It was fascinating, she'd discovered, to watch a film being put together. In principle, Ross was the producer, but she'd learned that he also had a hand in directing the films.

'Let's start off by letting the audience see the coral reef in the distance,' Ross said quietly, 'and the sheer drop to the sea. Then we can gradually move to the background of the pine forest and sweep down to a view of the lake, so that we see the sun shining on the surface.'

The cameraman nodded, and Ross went on, 'Lastly, I want you to bring in the bridge over the main road and try to give us an impression of the sheer height and majesty of it all. We'll tie all that in with atmospheric music and build up to a crescendo.'

'Okay. And that's where we cut to the car chase?'

'That's right. As soon as that comes to an end, we'll go straight into the stunt scene.'

'You want the lorry to come into the picture from the east? I'll need a clear signal for that.'

'Yes. I'll let you know as soon as the driver starts up the engine.'

'Okay.'

Alyssa watched all the activity around her with interest. The actors who would be needed for the next scene were standing around, chatting to one another, languid in the heat of the sun as they waited to be called. Everyone wanted to see how the stunt would go. The technicians had planned it down to the last detail, and there had been several rehearsals, but now it was time for the real thing, and the stuntman, Alex, was in position on the bridge, a lone, dark figure against the protective rail.

Ross came over to her. He was in prime form, bubbling with energy and totally enthusiastic about the way things were going. 'I'm going to be tied up with this for the next hour or so,' he told her, 'but I thought we might have lunch later at the new restaurant that's opened up in town… Benvenuto. It's down by the marina. They do some great dishes there. I think you'll like it.'

'Sounds great. I'll look forward to it.' Alyssa smiled at him and on the spur of the moment he wrapped his arms around her and kissed her soundly on the lips.

'Me, too.'

'Oh.' She was startled by the fervour that went into that kiss. 'What was that for?'

He grinned. 'I really appreciate what you've done here for us these last few weeks. Everyone says you've been brilliant, helping with everything from toothache to blistered toes. And I love the way you've looked over the script and offered advice on the medical stuff. Even if they're just a minor part of the film, it's important we get the hospital scenes right. And in the restaurant, when the man keels over, we needed to know how a doctor would respond.'

'Let's hope that won't be necessary at the restaurant today.' She laughed. 'It'll be great to sit and enjoy a meal in peace and quiet after all the goings-on on set.'

'Yeah, too right.' He gave her a final hug before letting her go. Then he hurried over to the lorry driver to give some final instructions.

'Going by the looks of things, it seems you and Ross are getting closer every day.' There was an edge to Connor's voice, and Alyssa looked at him in surprise as he came to stand beside her. His jaw was faintly clenched as though he was holding himself in restraint. He was wearing stone-coloured trousers and a casual, open-necked shirt, and he looked cool in the heat of the day.

'Hello, Connor,' she greeted him in a light tone, trying to counteract his disapproval. 'I wasn't expecting to see you here. I imagined you would be at work.' In fact, she'd seen very little of him these last few weeks, considering that they shared the same house, but she guessed he started work early at the hospital and he often came home late. Occasionally, he'd gone over to Florida to oversee his other project. Perhaps he'd been going out of an evening, too, once his shift ended.

As to his comment about her and Ross…she simply wasn't going to answer him. He was obviously hung up on the situation, so why make matters worse? It bothered her, though, that he had seen that kiss. How would she ever be able to convince him that there was nothing going on between her and his brother after that?

'It's my day off,' he said, 'so I thought I'd come and see how things were going here. Apparently the filming's on schedule so far.' His dark gaze moved over her. 'And I wondered how you were getting on. Has it been the quiet, relaxing time you expected?'

'Not exactly,' she murmured. 'But, then, I've been making something of an effort to get to grips with the job from the start.'

'Yes, so I heard.' A glimmer of respect flickered in the depths of his eyes. 'Ross has been singing your praises for days now. Apparently, you've made yourself known to everyone on set and managed to get a medical history from each one of them. He's very impressed with the way you've been handling things.'

Alyssa shrugged lightly, inadvertently loosening one of the thin straps of her broderie-anglaise top, so that it slid down the lightly tanned, silky smooth slope of her shoulder. 'It's what I'm paid to do, and the job is exactly what I thought it would be. I made it my business to get to know as much as I could about everyone beforehand so that I would have a good idea what I'm dealing with.'

'Very commendable.' Before she could remedy the offending strap, he reached out and hooked a finger beneath the cotton, carefully sliding it back into place. His touch trailed over her bare flesh like the slow lick of flame, causing an unexpected, feverish response to cascade through her, heating her blood and quickening her pulse.

'There,' he murmured. 'You're all neat and tidy once more.'

'I…um…have you…have you been to see every one of Ross's films being made?' she asked, disconcerted by his action and lifting a hand to push back the curls from her hot face. The movement lifted her brief top and exposed a small portion of her bare midriff, pale gold above the waistband of her dark jeans. His glance flicked downwards and lingered there for a while.

'I…uh…' He sounded distracted for a moment and then he cleared his throat. 'Most of them. I like to keep up with what's going on in the film world from time to time. Even though he's my brother, I must say Ross's work is good. He's had some notable successes. He deserves them because he works hard and pays a lot of attention to detail.'

She nodded. 'I've noticed that, too. He's been worrying about this morning's stunt, though. The timing has to be perfect. The stuntman has to jump from the bridge onto the moving lorry to escape from his pursuers, and he has to do it at exactly the right moment. They've even worked out how to make sure the lorry will be going at a certain speed when he jumps.'

He nodded. 'I guess that's what you might expect with these action adventure films. There always has to be something spectacular going on. After all, that's what the audience pays to see.'

Ross gave the signal for the camera recording to begin, and they turned to watch the proceedings. Around them, the buzz of conversation came to a halt and everyone's gaze was riveted to the scene about to take place. A lorry began to gradually pick up speed on the main road, which had been temporarily cleared of traffic while filming took place. The stuntman abandoned a wrecked car on the bridge and ran, chased determinedly by burly men who looked as though they meant business…nasty business. Coming to the concrete bulwark, he glanced around as though his character was trying to assimilate his options in double quick time.

With nowhere to go, and his pursuers gaining ground with every second that passed, he sprang up onto the guard-rail, remained poised for a moment, and then, as the men snapped at his heels, he leapt from the bridge.

The landing was perfect. He balanced, feet apart on top of the moving lorry, but a moment later a shocked gasp went up as the onlookers took in what happened next. Somehow Alex's foot twisted beneath him and the momentum of the still moving lorry flipped him onto his back, causing him to topple to the ground.

Alyssa was already on the move as it was happening, grabbing her medical equipment and racing towards the road where Alex was lying on the grass verge, groaning in agony. Her heart began to pound against the wall of her chest. This was the last thing she had expected. They'd been working so hard to make sure that nothing could go wrong. She had even checked him over to make sure that he was in prime physical condition before he attempted the feat.

'Alex, can you tell me where it hurts?' She quickly knelt down beside him, looking at him in concern.

'It's my back,' he said, his face contorted with pain. 'I think I caught it on the side of the lorry as I went over. I thought I felt something crack.'

The thought of the damage that might have been done to his spine made her sick with fear. All those old feelings of dread that she'd experienced back in the UK came flooding back to her, but she knew she had to get a grip on her emotions for her patient's sake. Small beads of perspiration broke out on her brow.

'Okay,' she said, disguising her inner fears with an air of confidence, 'try not to worry. We'll soon have you feeling more comfortable.' She dialled emergency services, calling for an ambulance and warning them of a suspected spinal injury, and then she turned to Alex once more. 'I just need to check you over to see what the damage is.' All the colour had drained from his face, but at least he was still conscious and able to talk to her. That was perhaps a good sign, but she'd seen the way he'd fallen, and it didn't bode well.

'I can't believe I…could have messed up like that,' Alex said in a taut, strained voice. 'I thought…I thought it was going to be okay…' He broke off, and small beads of perspiration broke out on his brow.

'Are you in a lot of pain?' she asked. 'On a scale of one to ten?'

'Twelve,' he said, squeezing his eyes closed and pushing the word out through his teeth.

'All right.' Her head was swimming—the shock of this awful event was beginning to crowd in on her, but she made a huge effort to cast her feelings to one side. 'I'll give you something to take that away, just as soon as I've done a preliminary examination. Try not to move. It's very important that you stay still.'

She made a brief but thorough check of his injuries and noted his blood pressure and pulse, before injecting him with a painkiller. 'I need to put a collar around your neck to immobilise it and make sure there'll be no further damage.'

Alex didn't answer her. His strength seemed to be ebbing away, and she realised that he might be slipping into neurogenic shock through a combination of pressure on the spinal cord and possible internal bleeding. A wave of panic swept through her. It was down to her to get him through this. What if she couldn't do it?

'Would you like some help?' Connor came over to her, and she guessed he'd been standing by, waiting to see if he was needed.

'Yes, that would be great, thanks.' Alyssa sent him a fleeting glance. His expression was serious, but he was calm, and his long, lean body was poised and ready for action. If only she could experience some of that inner composure. She said quietly, 'His blood pressure and pulse are both dropping rapidly, so I'm going to try to stabilise him with intravenous fluids.'

It was a very disturbing situation. When she tested his reflexes, Alex wasn't aware of any sensation in his legs and that was tremendously worrying, because it meant the eventual outcome could be disastrous. It was possible the damage was so great that Alex might never walk again.

She dashed those thoughts from her mind and breathed deeply to try to overcome the chaotic beat of her heart, concentrating on doing what she could for her patient. It was down to her to bring about the best outcome possible for him and the responsibility weighed heavily on her. 'I want to get a rigid collar around his neck…that's all important…and we must give him oxygen.'

He nodded. 'I'll do that for you.' He knelt down and supported Alex's neck while Alyssa carefully fixed the protective collar in place. Then he placed the oxygen mask over their patient's nose and mouth and started to squeeze the oxygen bag rhythmically. All the time, Alyssa was aware that Alex was slipping into unconsciousness.

She sucked in her breath. 'His heart rate is way too low. I'm going to give him atropine and have the defibrillator standing by, just in case.' Simply, if the heart didn't pump blood around his body effectively, her patient would die, but the atropine should help to increase the heart rate.

She quickly prepared the syringe while Connor continued with the oxygen. 'Okay,' she murmured, 'let's see if that will bring him round.' While they waited for the drug to work, Alyssa placed pads on Alex's chest and connected him to the portable defibrillator.

'It's not happening—the heart rate's not picking up enough,' Connor observed with a frown a short time later. 'Maybe it's time to deliver a shock to the heart.'

She nodded and set the machine to the correct rate and current. 'Stay clear of him while I do that.'

Connor moved back a little, and both of them waited. For a second or two, nothing happened, and Alyssa's mouth became painfully dry, the breath catching in her throat. She realised she was praying silently. This had to work.

Then there was a faint bleep, and the display on the defibrillator began to show a normal heart rhythm. She breathed a sigh of relief. The rate was still slow, but at least he was out of the woods for the moment.

The ambulance arrived as she and Connor continued the struggle to regulate Alex's blood pressure. The paramedics greeted Connor as a friend, as if they'd known him for a long time, and then they listened as Alyssa quickly brought them up to date with what was going on.

'I'm very worried about any injury to his back,' she said quietly, 'so we need to take great care when we move him. We'll help you to get him onto a spinal board.'

She and Connor knelt with one of the paramedics alongside Alex's still form, each one ready to lift and gently roll him on his side towards them on Alyssa's command. 'Okay, let's do it…three… two…one…go.'

The second paramedic slid the board underneath Alex, and then they carefully rolled him onto his back once more.

'That was well done.' Alyssa stood back as the paramedics strapped him securely in place and lifted him on to a trolley stretcher. Alex was still not speaking and she was dreadfully afraid his condition was deteriorating fast. 'I'll go with him to the hospital.'

'Okay.' The paramedic nodded and turned to Connor. 'Will you be coming along, too?'

'Yes. I'll follow in my car.'

Alyssa watched as they trundled Alex towards the ambulance, and saw, out of the corner of her eye, that Ross was hovering nearby. Seeing that she had finished working on her patient for the time being, he hurried over to her.

'Is he going to be all right? I couldn't believe what I was seeing. It's my worst nightmare.' The lively, boyish young man he'd been just a short time ago had disappeared completely. He looked haggard, devastated by what had happened.

'We'll know more after they've done tests at the hospital.' She laid a hand on his arm, wanting to comfort him. 'It wasn't your fault, Ross. All stunts carry danger, you know that. It was plain bad luck.'

'Even so, I feel terrible about it.' His face was ashen. 'Maybe I shouldn't have been directing today, but Dan had to be somewhere else, so I had to step in. I know he wanted to be here for this scene. Maybe it was an omen...'

'Ross, you mustn't blame yourself. No one could have foreseen what happened.'

His shoulders sagged. 'I don't know...I thought

I had everything covered…' He pulled himself together, straightening up. 'I want to go to the hospital to be with him, but I have to get in touch with his wife, and stay here and talk to the police, and try to explain what went wrong. There will be all sorts of questions, accident reports, insurance forms to be dealt with… I'm going to be sifting through all that over the next few hours, but tell him we'll take care of his family and see to anything that he needs, will you? Anything he wants, he just has to ask.'

'I'll tell him.'

'Thanks. I'll come along to see him just as soon as I can.'

'Of course.'

She gave him a reassuring hug and then turned back to the ambulance. Connor was standing by the open doors, supervising Alex's transfer.

'It looks as though Ross isn't taking it too well,' he murmured.

'No, he isn't. He feels responsible.' She glanced at him. He looked concerned as he watched his brother brace himself and walk towards a uniformed officer. 'Do you want to stay with him while he talks to the police and so on?'

He shook his head. 'No, I think I can probably be of more use at the hospital. I'm sure Ross will cope once he's over the initial shock.'

'Maybe. Let's hope so.' She frowned, rubbing absently at her temple, where a pulse had begun to throb.

He studied her, his grey eyes narrowing. 'Are you all right? You've gone very pale all of a sudden.'

'I'll be fine. It's just a bit of a headache starting.' She had to admit to herself, though, that now her role as an immediate response medic was complete, she wasn't feeling good at all. She'd taken this job feeling pretty certain that nothing like this would ever happen. When it had, despite all the odds, she'd found herself acting purely on instinct, following the basic tenets of medical care in the way that she'd been taught, in a way that had become second nature to her.

Now, to her dismay, the adrenaline that had kept her going through those initial moments was draining away and in the aftermath she was shaking inside. She was experiencing those same feelings of dread, of exhaustion and nervous tension that had started to overwhelm her when she had been working in emergency back home. A feeling of nausea washed over her.

She climbed into the ambulance and seated herself beside Alex, closing her eyes for a brief moment as though that would shut out the memories. He reminded her so much of that patient she'd treated back in the UK. They were about the same age, the same build, with dark hair and pain-filled eyes that haunted her, and both had fallen...

The paramedic closed the doors, bringing her back to the present with a jolt, and within a few seconds they were on their way, siren blaring, to the hospital.

Connor met them at the ambulance bay. 'Welcome to Coral Cay Hospital,' he murmured, reaching out to help Alyssa step down from the vehicle. His grip was firm and the hand at her elbow was reassuringly supportive. 'Our trauma team is all ready and waiting for the patient. They'll take good care of him, you'll see.'

Oddly, she was glad he had decided to come here with her. 'Yes, I'm sure they will.' By all accounts, the hospital had a good reputation and Alex would be in safe hands.

The registrar was already walking by the side of the trolley as the paramedics wheeled Alex into the emergency unit, and Alyssa went with them, ready to talk to the doctor about his condition.

'We'll do a thorough neurological examination,' the registrar told her. 'And then we'll get a CT scan done so that we can find out exactly what's going on.' He glanced at Connor. 'Do you know how we can get in touch with any of his relatives?'

Connor nodded. 'You don't need to worry about that, Jack. My brother's already spoken to Alex's wife. He rang to tell me on the car phone when I was on my way over here. She's going to make arrangements for someone to look after the children while she comes to be with him.'

'That's good.' They'd reached the trauma bay by now, and Jack started on his examination of the patient. Alyssa and Connor took turns to tell him what had happened and describe the treatment they had given Alex.

'You did everything you could,' the registrar said, 'but there's nothing more you can do here. Why don't you two go and get a cup of coffee, and I'll let you know as soon as the scans are finished? I know how concerned you must be, but I promise I'll keep you in the loop.'

'Okay. Thanks. We'll get out of your way.' Alyssa glanced at Alex, who was connected to monitors that bleeped and flashed and underlined the fact that he was in a distressing condition.

'I can hardly believe this is happening,' she said under her breath as she walked away with Connor.

He nodded. 'It's hard to take in.' He sent her an oblique glance. 'Are you okay? You don't look quite right.'

'I'm fine,' she lied.

'Hmm. I suppose all this must come as a shock

when you imagined the job would involve nothing more than having to deal with a few minor ailments or lacerations.' He led the way along the corridor and showed her to his office, pushing open the door and ushering her inside, his hand resting lightly on the small of her back. It was strangely comforting, that warmth of human contact.

'Please…take a seat.' He waved her to a chair by the desk, and then flicked a switch on the coffee machine that stood on a table in a corner of the room.

She looked around. The office had been furnished with infinite care, from the seagrass-coloured carpet that added a quiet dignity over all, to the elegantly upholstered leather armchairs that would provide comfort and ease to anxious relatives, keen to know the details of any treatment their loved ones would need. There was a leather couch, too, set against one wall, adding a feeling of opulence to the whole.

To one side of the room there was a mahogany bookcase, filled with leather bound medical books, and in front of the large window was a highly polished desk made of the same rich, dark mahogany. This was topped with a burgundy leather desk mat and beautiful accessories, which included a brass pen-holder and an intricately designed brass paperweight.

'You're still look very white-faced,' he remarked as he set out two cups and saucers and began to pour coffee. 'It's not just that you're worried about Alex, is it? I can't help thinking there's something more.' He hesitated for a moment. 'Shall I get you some painkillers for the headache?'

She shook her head. 'Like I said, I'll be fine.'

He slid a cup towards her. 'Would you like cream and sugar with that?'

'Please.' She nodded, and he slid a tray containing a cream jug and sugar bowl onto the desk beside her. The bowl was filled with amber-coloured chips of rock sugar that gleamed softly in the sunlight and gave off a pleasing aroma of dark molasses.

Connor sat down, leaning back in his black

leather chair, eyeing her over the rim of his cup. 'Something's definitely not right,' he said. 'What is it? You did all you possibly could for Alex, so it can't be that. Does it have something to do with the reason you're not working back in the UK?'

Her eyes widened and her heart missed a beat. 'Why would you think that?'

He shrugged. 'A few stray connections linking up in my mind. It's odd that you would leave the place where you did your training and where you worked for several years and give it all up to come halfway across the world. I can't help thinking something must have gone wrong. It's not as though you could afford to travel the world and simply take time out.'

She raised a brow. 'How do you know all that? Have you been talking to Ross?'

He smiled. 'Of course. He talks about you every opportunity he gets.'

'Oh, dear.' She brooded on that for a moment or two. She'd never given Ross the slightest encouragement to think of her as anything more than a friend, but somewhere along the way he must have started pinning his hopes on something more developing between them. Judging by what Connor was saying, she would have to put a stop to it, and sooner rather than later.

He was watching her as she thought things through. 'He thinks the world of you and would do anything for you, but we both know that you don't really feel the same way about him, don't we?'

She stiffened. 'I like Ross. I think he's a wonderful person.' She didn't appreciate the faintly challenging note in Connor's tone. It annoyed her that he should imply she had come here with an ulterior motive.

'Yes, he is…' Connor agreed, 'but that still doesn't explain why you abandoned everything to come out here with him.'

She sipped her coffee, giving herself time to gain a little more composure. 'You think I was sick of working for a living and gave up on it to follow him, don't you?'

'Isn't that a possibility?' He studied her thoughtfully. 'The idea of coming to a sun-soaked island where you could relax and forget your cares must have had huge appeal.'

She smiled briefly. 'Of course it did. But you're forgetting…in my case I'm actually here to work. Ross gave me the opportunity to try something new and I jumped at it. I don't see anything wrong with that. Do you?' Her chin lifted and a hint of defiance shimmered in her green eyes.

'When you put it that way, no…of course not.' His glance wandered over her face, lingering on the perfect curve of her mouth, the fullness of her lips made moist by the coffee and accentuated by the inviting, cherry-red lipstick she was wearing. After a moment or two he pulled himself up and shook his head as though to clear it. 'I dare say a lot of people would envy you being able to simply take off and leave everything behind.'

'I guess so.' She might have said more, but his pager went off just then, and he frowned as he checked the text message. 'Jack Somers has finished the preliminary tests. We can go and talk to him now.'

'That's good.' Her stomach muscles tightened in nervous expectation.

They went to find the registrar in his office. 'I have the CT scans here,' he said, bringing up the films on his computer screen. 'You'll see there are a couple of fractured vertebrae and there's a lot of inflammation around that area.'

Connor winced. 'It'll mean an operation, then?'

Jack nodded. 'I'm afraid so.' He glanced at Alyssa. 'We'll get him prepped for surgery as soon as possible, maybe within the hour. The surgeon will stabilise the spine with metal rods and screws and do what he can to ease the pressure on the spinal cord. Unfortunately, it'll be some time before we know what the outcome will be regarding him regaining any movement in his legs. There's so much swelling that it's hard to see exactly what damage has been done.'

'I appreciate that. Thanks for letting us know.' Alyssa was saddened, looking at those films. How would Alex take the news, having been an active, athletic man? He was in his prime, with a young family to support, and it grieved her to think of how this would affect them.

Connor added his thanks and they left the office, going over to the trauma room where Alex was being tended by two specialist nurses. Alyssa spoke to them and watched for a while as they set up drips and programmed the medication pump. He was still unresponsive, but he was being well looked after, she felt sure.

There was nothing more they could do there and she went with Connor to the car park a few minutes later.

'Time's slipping by faster than I imagined,' he said, looking briefly at the gold watch on his wrist. 'Maybe we should go and get some lunch and come back later to see how he's doing once the operation is over.' He glanced at her. 'We could go to Benvenuto, if you like. It would be a shame to let Ross's lunch reservations go to waste, don't you think?'

'I don't know. I...' His offer caught her unawares. Until that moment she hadn't even realised she was hungry, but now he mentioned it there was a definite hollow feeling in her stomach. Even so, it made her feel uncomfortable to think of deserting Ross and going out to lunch with Connor instead. 'Is there no chance he could join us? Perhaps I should give him a call...'

'I already did that.' They had reached his car, a low-slung, highly polished sports model, and now he pulled open the passenger door and waited for her to slide onto the leather upholstered seat. 'I spoke to him while you were talking to the nurses. He agreed it would be a shame to let the booking go to waste.'

'Oh, I see.' She frowned. 'I suppose he's still busy dealing with the accident reports? Did he say how it was going?'

'He's still talking to the insurers and working on his report. Then at some point he'll have to meet with the director and work out how they can reschedule the filming. Everything's been put on hold for the next couple of days. Everybody's too upset to go on right now. He's spoken to Alex's wife, and arranged for a car to take her to the hospital.'

'I'm glad he did that.'

Connor slid into the driver's seat and set the car in motion, while Alyssa sat back, thankful for the air-conditioning on such a hot day. Connor had a light touch on the controls and it seemed as though the car was a dream to handle, smooth and responsive, covering the miles with ease. If it hadn't been for her worries, the journey to the marina would have been soothing and a delight to savour.

Instead, she tried to take her mind off things by looking out of the window at the landscape of hills clad with pine forest, which soon receded into the distance and changed to a vista of lush orange groves and thriving banana plantations.

'We're almost there,' Connor said a little later, pointing out the blue waters of the marina in the distance. 'I expect the place will be quite busy at this time of the day, but Ross reserved a table on the terrace, so we'll be in the best spot and able to look out over the yacht basin.'

'That sounds great.' She made a face. 'I'm actually starving. I hadn't realised it was so long since breakfast.'

'Hmm. I'm not surprised.' He looked her over and smiled. 'I doubt you can really give what you have to eat the term "breakfast". Fruit juice and a small bowl of cereal is more like a quick snack, I'd say.'

She looked at him in astonishment as he drove into the restaurant car park. 'What do you mean? How do you know what I eat?'

He slipped the car into a parking space and cut the engine. 'I've seen you from the upper deck—you often go out onto the terrace to eat first thing in the morning, don't you? You're a lot like me in that. I like to be out in the fresh air so that I can take stock of my surroundings and, like you, I drink freshly squeezed orange juice. It makes me feel good first thing in the morning. Though how you can expect to last for long on what you eat is beyond me.'

He came around to the passenger side of the car and opened the door for her. She frowned. 'I usually take a break mid-morning and catch up with a bun or a croissant,' she said in a rueful tone. 'Of course, with everything going on the way it did today, that didn't happen.'

'You should enjoy the food here all the more, then.' He locked the car and laid a hand on the small of her back, leading her into the restaurant.

Alyssa was glad of the coolness of the interior. His casual, gentle touch felt very much like a caress to her heightened senses, and the heat it generated seemed to suffuse her whole body.

A waiter showed them to their table out on the terrace, and once again the heat of the sun beat down on Alyssa's bare arms. Her cheeks felt flushed and Connor must have noticed because he said softly, 'At least we'll be in the shade of that palm tree. There's a faint breeze sifting through the branches—couldn't be better.'

'It's lovely here.' She sat down and absorbed the beauty of her surroundings for a while until gradually she felt herself begin to relax. On one side there was the marina, with an assortment of yachts bobbing gently on the water, and on the other there was the sweep of the beach, with a magnificent stretch of soft, white sand and a backdrop of low scrub and palm trees.

In the distance, the coastline changed yet again, becoming rocky, with jagged inlets, peninsulas and lagoons. There, the trees were different, smaller, and she could just about make out their twisting trunks and branches laden with sprays of yellow flowers. 'Are those the logwood trees I've been hearing about?' she asked, and he nodded.

'That's right.'

'I heard the wood yields a rich, deep reddish-purple dye,' she said. 'I've seen some lovely silk garments that were coloured with it.'

'Yes, it's used quite widely hereabouts. The flowers give great honey, too, so I guess it's a useful tree all round.'

The waiter handed them menus, and they were silent for a moment, studying them. Connor ordered a bottle of wine.

'I can't make up my mind what to choose,' Alyssa said after a while. 'Everything looks mouth-wateringly good to me.'

'I thought I might start with conch chowder and follow it with shrimp Alfredo and marinara-flavoured pasta,' he murmured. 'They do those dishes particularly well here.'

'Hmm…I think I'll go along with that, too.' She smiled and laid down her menu.

The waiter took their orders, and Connor poured her a glass of wine and asked about her family back home.

'Do you have any relatives in the UK? I know you have your cousin Carys in Florida.'

'My parents are living in London at the moment,' she told him. 'I don't have any brothers or sisters.'

He frowned. 'I imagine they must miss you, the more so since you're an only child.'

'Possibly.' She thought about that for a moment or two. 'But they're really quite busy… My mother runs a boutique and my father is a businessman, a director of an electronics company. I don't think they'll really have time to worry about what I'm getting up to. And of course I've lived away from home for a number of years, since I qualified as a doctor.'

'Hmm…that sounds like quite a…sterile…relationship.' He studied her for a while, pausing the conversation as the waiter brought a tureen of chowder to the table and began to ladle it into bowls.

Alyssa tasted her creamy soup and mulled over Connor's remark. 'I don't know about that,' she said. 'It was always that way, for as long as I can remember. In my teenage years I was what people called a latchkey kid, coming home to an empty house because my parents worked late. I didn't mind back then. In fact, I never thought much about it. I learned to fend for myself, and there were always friends that I could be with, so I wasn't lonely.'

He'd hit on something, though, the way he'd described her relationship with her family. Her eyes were troubled as she thought it over. Sometimes she'd missed that intimacy of family closeness that her friends had seemed to take for granted, especially when her career had started falling apart and her love life had taken a dive. She hadn't felt able to share her innermost secrets, even with her best friends, but it would have been good to be able to turn to family in her hour of need.

She told him a little about her mother's fashionable boutique, and how she would try on the latest designs and try to persuade her mother that she could be a good advert for the shop by wearing the beautiful creations.

'She didn't fall for that one very often, unfortunately.' She smiled, and hesitated while the waiter cleared away the first course. 'Do your parents live close by?' she asked.

He nodded. 'Reasonably so. They live in the Bahamas, but on different islands. I see them quite often, but never actually together. They divorced some years ago and my father remarried recently.'

'I'm sorry.' She frowned. 'It must have been hard for you to cope with that…for Ross, too.'

'Yes. It was difficult for Ross, especially. He was about eleven at the time, and very impressionable. Of course, you grow up hoping that your parents will stay together for ever, and when it doesn't work out that way you struggle to come to terms with all the fallout.'

'I understand how that must be a problem.' Her gaze was sympathetic. 'I've been lucky, I suppose, in that my parents are still together.'

The main course arrived, and they were quiet for a while, savouring the delicate flavours of pasta and shrimp, and then they both marvelled at the way the chef had brought his magic touch to the ingredients. The pasta was made with tomatoes, garlic and herbs, and was particularly good.

'I can see why this place is so popular,' Alyssa murmured, spearing a shrimp with her fork and raising it to her lips. 'This is delicious.' She loved the flavour of the Alfredo sauce, made from a blend of white sauce and cream cheese.

Connor watched her, his glance following the gentle sweep of her hand and hovering around the full curve of her mouth. He topped up her glass with wine, a light, fruity complement to the superb food.

'It is,' he agreed softly. 'But, you know, there are lots of good experiences to be had on our island. Sightseeing, sailing, maybe even exploring the coral reefs…though I expect you know all about those.' He lifted his glass and swallowed some of the clear liquid. 'Have you had time to look around and get to know the place?'

She shook her head, causing the bright curls to quiver and drift against her shoulders. 'Not yet, unfortunately. Ross wanted to show me around, but he's been very busy with the film, and for my part I'm still trying to get settled in and find my way around my new job. I dare say there will be time to do all those other things before too long. I have a couple more months on my contract here, so there's no hurry.'

'I could take you anywhere you wanted to go,' he suggested. 'It would be a shame to miss out on any of the delights of this beautiful island, don't you think?' His voice was silky smooth, reassuringly pleasant and somehow intimate at the same time.

'I…uh…yes, I suppose so.' Alarm bells started to ring inside her head. His offer was tempting, but why was he offering to show her around? He'd made it quite plain where they stood, on two sides of a dividing line, with Ross in between. 'Um…it's great of you to offer, but you really don't have to put yourself out.' She returned his gaze. 'I'm sure Ross will be free soon enough to take me out and about, and even if he isn't, I can manage some sightseeing by myself.'

'But that wouldn't be quite as enjoyable, I think.' He leaned back in his chair as the waiter came to clear the table and take their order for dessert. He handed her the menu. 'What's your fancy? There are all sorts of dishes flavoured with coconut—as you might imagine, with the number of palm trees around—or bananas, of course. Or maybe you prefer chocolate?'

'Do you know, I think I'd like to try the crêpes Suzette. Have you tried them?'

'I have. They're a good choice. I think I'll join

you. One of their specialties here is to bring them to the table and flame them in Curaçao and Grand Marnier and then top them with luscious, sweet, dark cherries.' He smiled and gave the order to the waiter, then offered to top up her wine glass once more.

She covered the glass with her hand. 'No more for me, thanks. I need to keep a clear head.'

'Why do you have to do that? You're not on duty any more, are you? Filming has stopped for a couple of days, so you can relax for a while. Why not take the opportunity to ease back from work and being on your guard?' His dark eyes seemed to glint as he spoke, but it might have been a trick of the light. 'Because you are on your guard, aren't you?' he murmured.

With him, yes, she'd been constantly on her guard, ever since the moment they'd first met. He knew it, and she couldn't help but feel he was tormenting her with the knowledge.

'I've always found it best to keep an eye on what's going on all around,' she said quietly. She'd been caught unawares with James, her ex-boyfriend, and she was determined nothing like that was ever going to happen again.

'Hmm…I wonder why?' His eyes narrowed on her, but she didn't answer him.

Instead, she took an interest in the dessert dish that the waiter prepared with a flourish before placing it in front of her. She dipped in a spoon and tasted the mix of flavours. The crêpe Suzette was hot, with a melt-in-the-mouth sauce, and the smooth, cold ice cream served with it was a delicious contrast. Connor watched her for a moment, as though he was fascinated by her absorption with the food.

'We both have some free time outside work,' he murmured, 'so perhaps you could think again about us spending it together… Maybe we could take a trip on a glass-bottomed boat so that you can see the coral close at hand. Would you like that?'

'I'm sure it would be a delightful experience,' she said softly, and he lifted a dark brow in expectation until she added, 'but somehow I don't think it would be right for you and me to be to-gether too much outside work.'

'You don't?' He studied her thoughtfully, tak-ing time to taste his dessert. 'Why is that? Are you afraid Ross might be concerned about what you're doing?'

'Not exactly…but I'm a bit puzzled. After all, if you really think there's something going on be-tween us, it's a bit strange that you would think of asking me out.' She finished off her dessert and laid down her spoon, resting her hand on the table alongside her wine glass and running the tips of her fingers over the delicate stem.

He shrugged. 'I heard you say that you were through with romance, so maybe I'm taking that statement at face value. In that case, why should it be a problem for Ross if you and I were to spend some time together?' He reached for her hand, taking it into his palm and brushing his thumb lightly over her smooth skin. Her heart began to thump heavily.

'I'd like to spend time with you, Alyssa, and get to know you better.'

'Like I said, I don't think that would be a very good idea.' Her voice was husky, drowned out by the thunder of the blood in her veins as his fingers travelled along her wrist in a subtle caress. 'I…uh…I'm not looking for any kind of involvement right now.'

'That's all right. Neither am I. Things don't have to get serious. I'm not looking for commitment.' His mouth made a wry curve. 'After the mess my parents made of things, that's the last thing I'm looking for.' His gaze meshed with hers. 'But we could have a good time all the same, you and I…no strings.'

She made a faint smile. 'That sounds…interesting,' she murmured, the breath catching in her throat. Her heart had switched into overdrive now, the beat building up to a crescendo as his fingers gently massaged the back of her hand and his thumb made tantalising circles over her wrist. 'Only…' She pulled in a deep breath. 'Only I have the feeling you're not being quite straight with me. I did mean what I said. I'm not looking for any kind of attachment right now, strings or no strings.'

She carefully extracted her hand from his. 'I'm sorry if that messes with your plans.'

He frowned. 'Not at all. It was just a suggestion, and I don't want to upset you in any way.' His glance drifted over her. 'Can you blame me for trying? You're a beautiful young woman, and I'd surely need to have ice water in my veins if I wasn't interested in you.'

She swallowed hard. 'I'm flattered, I think, but my answer's still the same, I'm afraid. I'd sooner keep things the way they are.'

'As you please, of course.' He smiled. 'Though that's not to say I won't keep trying.'

He signalled to the waiter to bring coffee, and for the rest of their time at the restaurant he was charm itself, talking to her about the island, the people and places that made up its exotic appeal. He backed off from making any more overtures and she tried to relax a little.

She didn't believe for one minute that he was interested in her for her own sake. No matter what he said, he was acting purely in his brother's interests. He thought she was involved with him in some way, and he wanted to break it up, even if it meant taking her on himself. If Ross were to be hurt in the process, then so be it, because in his mind she was the dangerous one here.

He believed she had the power to ruin his brother's happiness, and he meant to put a stop to that by any means possible. She would be as wary of Connor as she would be of a stalking tiger.

CHAPTER THREE

'I CAN'T believe we've had such a difficult day.' Ross waited while Alyssa stopped to pick up the local newspaper that lay on the porch, tossed there by the delivery boy earlier in the afternoon.

Ross followed her along the hallway and into the spacious living room. 'Do you mind if I open the doors onto the veranda?'

'Please do. Open every one you come across.' She shrugged off her light cotton jacket and kicked off her shoes. It was early evening and she was looking forward to sitting out on the deck for a while. 'I'll fix us a drink. Would you like hot or cold?'

'Cold, definitely. All I want to do is to sprawl in a chair and wind down for half an hour or so.' He ran a hand through his dark hair, leaving it dishevelled and giving him a distinctly youthful appearance.

Alyssa looked at the newspaper, scanning the headlines, and winced. 'It says here there was an accident on the highway this morning. I wonder if Connor had to deal with that? I expect he must have, unless the casualties were flown to the mainland.'

The standard of driving out here could be atrocious, she'd discovered, with people speeding and driving recklessly, or overloading their vehicles to the point where they were dangerous. According to the news report, this latest crash was as the result of a motorcyclist weaving through lanes of moving traffic.

'He most probably did,' Ross said. 'In fact, he might have been called out to go to the scene—he does regular stints as an on-call first attender. The emergency services want him there if the injuries are very serious and it's something the paramedics can't deal with on their own.' He frowned. 'I'll give him a ring,' Ross said, 'if that's all right with you? I think I heard him moving about upstairs. I want to speak to him, anyway, to see how things are going, so I expect he'll want to come down here for a while.'

She nodded. 'That's okay. I'd better set out three glasses and some sandwiches.' She didn't feel that she had much choice but to see Connor, given that she was living in his house rent-free for the duration of her contract. To object would simply be churlish, wouldn't it? Her head was aching already, though, and the last thing she needed was to be on her guard around Connor.

He walked out on to the veranda a few minutes later, bringing with him a basket of fruit. 'For you,' he told Alyssa. 'I thought you might like to sample some of the fruits of our island.'

'Wow, that's quite an assortment,' she said in an appreciative tone, gazing down at the beautifully arranged wicker basket. 'There must be almost a dozen different types of fruit in here. Thank you for this.' She was impressed. Among them there were mangoes, papaya and green sugar apples, along with pears and a large, golden pineapple. 'I don't know what I've done to deserve this.'

'You didn't have to do anything at all. Think of it as a delayed welcome-to-the-island present, if you like.'

'I will. Thanks.' She was thoughtful for a moment or two. 'Perhaps I ought to take something like this along to the hospital when I go to see Alex.'

'He already has one.' Connor's expression became sombre. 'I had one made up for him and took it in to him this morning. He's not really very interested in anything, though, at the moment. He's very depressed.'

'I suppose it doesn't help that he's not able to move much at the moment, but at least the operation went well,' Alyssa murmured. 'It's just a question of taking time to heal now, isn't it? And he'll have physiotherapy, of course, once he's up to it.' She sent Connor a fleeting glance. 'I'm surprised you found the time to look in on him if the evening paper is anything to go by. It looks as though you had to deal with a nasty traffic accident.'

He pulled a face. 'Yes, it was pretty bad. There

were a few people involved, with some severe fractures, and the motorcyclist is in a very worrying condition. He went into cardiac arrest at the scene, but we managed to pull him through and get his heart started again. It's touch and go for him at the moment.'

'I'm sorry.' She frowned. 'It's a difficult job. You do what you can to patch people up, but the downside is that some of them don't make it.' Working in the emergency unit back in the UK, she had seen more than her fair share of traumatic injuries. Dealing with them day in and day out had become more than she could handle, especially when things hadn't gone well for the patient. She'd tried her utmost to help them, but occasionally fate had been against her, and that had been really hard to take.

She put down the basket of fruit in the kitchen and carried a tray out onto the deck, where they sat around on wicker chairs by a glass-topped table. She'd made up a jug of iced fruit juice and put out plates alongside a selection of sandwiches.

'Help yourselves,' she said, coming to sit down

in one of the chairs. She reached for one of the filled glasses, then leaned back and stretched out her long, bare legs. Her cool, cotton skirt draped itself just above her knees. 'Mmm…this is good,' she murmured, taking a long swallow. She held the glass against her hot forehead, letting the coolness soothe her aching head.

'It looks as though you've had a difficult day, too,' Connor remarked, pulling up a chair beside her. He wore light-coloured trousers that moulded themselves to his strong thighs, and a short-sleeved shirt that was open at the neck to reveal an expanse of lightly tanned throat. His arms were strong, well muscled, the forearms covered with a light sprinkling of dark hair. For some inexplicable reason his overwhelmingly masculine presence disturbed her, and she quickly looked away.

'You name it, everything went wrong today,' she murmured wearily. 'First of all part of the prefabricated set collapsed, causing some minor injuries, and then there was a problem with some of the actors getting sick. They'd been out to breakfast early this morning and were violently ill a few hours later—gastroenteritis, I think. I gave them rehydration salts and sent them home.'

'So now we're going to be even further behind schedule,' Ross put in. 'Tempers were fraying and everyone was in a bad mood...all except Alyssa, that is.' He smiled as he looked at her. 'Somehow she managed to stay serene and patient through it all. She's a very calming influence all round.'

He sat down in a chair opposite them, by the rail on the veranda, close to the shrubbery where bougainvillea bloomed, its glorious, deep pink, paper-thin flowers bright in the sunshine. They had been planted all around the property, between showy hibiscus and the pretty, trumpet-like yellow allamanda flowers.

'We managed to keep most of the film footage where Alex did the stunt scene, which was a relief.' He frowned. 'That sounds awful, me talking like that, doesn't it, seeing how ill he is, but it could have set us back really badly. As it is, that's one worry at least off our minds.'

'Are you having problems, then?' Connor asked. 'Apart from the scenery collapsing, I mean.' He made a wry smile.

'Like Alyssa said…you name it. Nothing's going right. It's as though the whole thing is jinxed. Everything that can go wrong is going wrong. Next thing you know, we'll not be able to shoot tomorrow because there'll be a hitch with the outdoor schedule we've set up.'

'Hmm…' Connor appeared to be turning things over in his head. 'That reminds me, I had a call from Dan a short time ago. He's been trying to get hold of you but your mobile was switched off, or something.'

Ross frowned, and checked his phone. 'Wouldn't you credit it?' he said with a grimace. 'Battery's flat.'

Connor acknowledged that with a slight inclination of his head. 'Actually, he said he wanted to meet up with you at the studio. He just got in today from Florida and he wants to talk to you about the filming. He said he'll be at the studio for another couple of hours.'

Ross sighed. 'I guess that puts paid to my evening of relaxation.' He took a couple of sandwiches from the plate and stood up. 'Thanks for
these, Alyssa,' he said. 'It looks as though I'll
have to eat them on the move.'

Alyssa watched him go, and then looked at
Connor with narrowed eyes. 'Was it really es-
sential that he had to go over there right now?
Surely a phone call would have done?'

Connor lifted his shoulders in a negligent fashion. 'I'm just the messenger,' he said. 'Far be it
from me to interfere with the day-to-day work
of the producer and the director.'

She looked at him from under her dark lashes.
There was a smile hovering around his mouth
and she didn't trust him an inch. She had the
strongest feeling that he had manoeuvred the situation so Ross didn't get to spend the evening
with her.

Her own phone rang just then, and she excused
herself for a while, going into the living room to
answer it. 'It's Carys,' she told Connor, as she
glanced at the name displayed on the screen.

'Help yourself to sandwiches and salad, and there are cheese and biscuits in the kitchen if you want them.'

'Thanks.'

She handed him the evening paper, and left him to look over the headlines while she went to speak to Carys.

Some ten minutes later she went back out onto the deck, the headache considerably worse, and her mood decidedly fractious.

Connor sent her a sideways glance. 'It doesn't look as though your cousin managed to cheer you up,' he commented. 'Just the opposite, I'd say.'

She gave him a tight-lipped smile. 'She was just giving me the news from back home. She's in touch with friends over there, and they help her keep up with the latest gossip.'

'It wasn't good news, though, judging from your expression.'

'Nothing bad. My parents are as busy as ever. Apparently my father is thinking of expanding the business, and my mother has a fashion show coming up in the next couple of weeks, where she'll be able to parade some of the latest styles she has on sale.'

'That's good, isn't it?'

'I guess so.' It would perhaps explain why they hadn't had time to return her calls or answer her emails.

'Is there something more? You seem tense.'

'Nothing important,' she said. She wasn't going to tell him about James, her ex. He'd been asking after her, apparently, wanting to know how he might get in touch. That was the last thing she wanted.

She sat down and drank more of the fruit juice. 'It's another niggling headache,' she told him when he continued to subject her to a brooding stare. 'I suppose I need to learn to relax a bit more and not let things get to me so easily.'

'That would be sensible, if you could take your own advice.' He gave her a faint smile, adding on a thoughtful note, 'You could try some of the local bush medicine. That might do the trick. Do you know about the tamarind tree?'

She shook her head.

He looked around. 'See that tree over there…?' He pointed to a tree a short distance away. It had attractive leaves that billowed in the slight breeze, and there were large, reddish-coloured seedpods hanging in clusters from the branches. She nodded.

'The natives call it the jumbie plant,' he said. 'It's another name for the tamarind. You collect the leaves and boil them up in water, and then let the mixture infuse for a while. When it's cool, you drink the brew. It's supposed to make you feel much better.'

'Hmm. That sounds interesting.' She frowned. 'I wonder if it works.'

He chuckled. 'Then again, you could save yourself all that bother and just take a couple of aspirin.'

She laughed with him, and he said quietly, 'Why don't we take a stroll on the beach for a while? It might help to make you feel better. You're probably just wound up after a stressful day.'

'Yes, you could be right about that.' A walk on

the beach sounded inviting, and before she gave the matter any more thought she found herself nodding. 'Okay. I think I'd enjoy a walk in the fresh air.'

She went to fetch her sandals from the sitting room, but draped the straps over her fingers as she walked barefoot along the white sand. The sun was beginning to set, casting a golden glow over the horizon, and the wading birds had come down to the shore, getting in a last meal before they retired for the night. Close by, humming birds flitted among the yellow elder flowers, sipping the nectar, and the sweet smell of frangipani filled the air. It was a magical time and Alyssa began to relax, watching the waves break on the shore, leaving behind small ribbons of white foam.

'I love this time of the day,' Connor said softly. 'Everything seems so peaceful and I find all the cares of the day begin to seep away. There's something very calming about coming down here to watch the ocean roll over the sand.'

'Mmm…that's true. I think it's because it's so

steadfast. We're busy running around chasing our tails, but the forces of nature stay the same throughout, the ocean ebbs and flows and day follows night, come what may.'

They walked along the shoreline, and Alyssa felt the warm wash of water bathe her feet. Connor joined her, going barefoot by her side, so that their feet left prints in the damp sand.

As they moved further along the beach, he reached for her hand, enclosing her fingers in his palm, and at the same time he put a finger to his mouth, indicating that they should fall silent. Then he pointed ahead and she saw what he was focusing on. It was a bird, standing almost two feet high, black with a white underbelly and a large, orange bill.

'What is he?' she whispered. 'I wish I knew more about the wildlife out here.'

'He's an American oystercatcher,' he said softly, 'looking for clams or mussels, I expect. The birds migrate here in the late summer, but I've not seen any around here for a while. I think this one's a juvenile, judging from the black tip of his bill.'

'It's fascinating to see it,' she whispered back, standing still so as not to cause any disturbance that would make the bird fly off. 'I've seen so many gorgeous tropical species since I've been here.'

He smiled, drawing her close and sliding his arm around her. 'I guessed you were interested in nature from that first day. That's why I wanted to bring you down here. I know you've been busy of an evening, with one thing and another, and you haven't had time to venture very far.' His hand rested on the curve of her hip, warm, coaxing, inviting her to lean into him, to nestle into the shelter of his long body.

She was sorely tempted to do that. Here on the balmy Caribbean shore, with the sun low in the sky and nothing but the intermittent call of birds to fill the air, anything was possible. And yet it was strange that she should feel this way, considering that she was cautious now about getting close to any man. With Connor, though, everything seemed different. He confused her and set her at war within herself.

Now, as he held her with gentle, natural intimacy, she felt mesmerised by him, as though it would be the simplest thing in the world to turn in his arms and give herself up to the sheer joy of his caresses. It was what she wanted, and that was bewildering because it was as though her mind and her body were totally unconnected, her body responding to his embrace with a will of its own.

His touch was smooth, gentle, gliding over her body with infinite care. His hand trailed a path over the swell of her hip, along her waist, enticing her to him with persuasive, hypnotic ease.

She looked up into his eyes. They were dark, engrossed in her, his smile reflected in the shimmering depths. Slowly, his head bent towards her and she knew what he was about to do and for the life of her she had no will to stop it. He was going to kiss her, and it would be everything she dreamed it would be, and a whole new world would open up for her…a world with Connor at its centre.

How could that be? She gave herself a mental

shake and put up a hand, flat against his chest. 'I can't,' she said softly. 'I just can't.'

'Alyssa…' Her name was a gentle sigh on his lips. 'You and I could be so good together. There's a chemistry between us…you know it and I know it. What would be the harm?'

'It's not right. It doesn't feel right. And besides, there's Ross… I can't do that to him.'

She felt as though she was taking Ross's name in vain, but Ross was the only safeguard she had. No matter that there wasn't anything between them, it was enough that Connor would have to think twice about what he was doing. Through all this, he had his brother's interests at heart.

'You don't want him,' he said huskily. 'You've been overwhelmed by the chance he gave you to come out here. Who wouldn't be? But if you're honest with yourself, you'll see that you want what he can give you… the kudos of being with a film producer, with a wealthy man, a man who can make all your cares disappear.'

His hand stroked along the length of her spine, a slow sweep of silk that made her insides quiver and fired up her blood so that her pulse throbbed and her heart hammered against her rib cage.

'You and I are a lot alike, though you may not see it right now. Think about it. We could make a go of it, have a good time, with no commitment on either side. It'll be fun, you'll see, if only you're brave enough to give it a try.'

She shook her head and took a step away from him. 'No, Connor,' she said. 'Forget it. It isn't going to happen.'

She swivelled around and started to walk back along the beach. She'd been badly hurt back home by James, who had sworn that he loved her, wanted her, needed her, and it had all ended in disaster.

She wasn't going to let that happen all over again, especially with a man who was only playing games with her heart.

CHAPTER FOUR

'HEY, look at you…you're absolutely gorgeous!' Ross exclaimed, his grey-blue eyes lighting up as Alyssa came out onto the deck. He gave a low whistle. 'You are fantastic.'

She gave him an uncertain smile. 'Well…thank you, but it's just a cocktail dress. I wasn't sure what I should wear for our evening out. Is this a bit over the top for a few drinks at a bar, do you think?'

'No way. But I can see I shall have to be on my guard—you'll turn the head of every man in the place.'

She made a wry smile. 'That's not exactly what I had in mind.' Ross was full of enthusiasm, and didn't seem to have noticed her worried expression. 'I just wanted to pick out something that's a little dressy to go along with the nature of the place and yet casual enough for an evening with friends.' She frowned. 'Now I'm not so sure I've made the right choice.'

'You have, believe me.' A soft, thudding sound caught their attention and they turned to see Connor climbing the steps onto the deck. 'Tell her, Connor,' Ross said. 'You must have heard what we were saying. Tell her she looks great.'

Connor was already looking at her, his eyes widening a fraction, but he didn't say anything for a second or two. He'd just arrived home from the hospital, and she could see by his expression that it had been a difficult day for him. There were lines of strain around his eyes and mouth, lending his strong features a trace of vulnerability.

He dragged his gaze away from her and nodded. 'You've pitched it just right,' he said at last. 'I'm assuming Ross is taking you to the Reef?'

'That's right.' Perversely, she didn't know whether to be disappointed or thankful that he'd made no other comment about how she looked. She was wearing a dress that faithfully followed the outline of her curves, an off-the-shoulder style, with a lightly beaded top and a skirt that finished just above her knees. 'We're having a get-together for the cast and crew, a sort of half-time rallying call. After everything that has gone wrong lately, Ross felt we needed some kind of pick-me-up.'

Connor nodded, coming to lean negligently against the rail. He looked good, dressed in pristine, dark trousers and a mid-blue linen shirt. 'Sounds good to me, but I'm not sure this is the best time to be going.'

She frowned. 'Why not? I don't know what you mean.'

'There's a storm brewing.' He looked up into the cloud-laden sky. 'I can feel it in the air. The heat was oppressive earlier, and now there's a change in the atmosphere. The wind's building up.'

Ross shook his head. 'It's a beautiful evening. There's just a bit of a breeze, that's all, and there have been no warnings issued. Anyway, we'll only be out for two or three hours. We all have to work in the morning.'

'Even so...' Connor stood his ground.

Alyssa sent Ross a troubled glance. 'It's not too late for us to cancel, is it, just to be sure?' For some reason she trusted Connor's judgement, and if he was cautious, perhaps they ought to take his concerns seriously. 'We could ring round and let everyone know, couldn't we? We can easily arrange a different date.'

'It's too late for that, I think,' Ross said. 'Some people will already be there. Besides, I don't think there's anything to worry about. The wind's coming in off the sea, it's true, and it feels a little chillier than we're used to, but it'll be fine, I'm sure. We might get a heavy rainstorm, but it should blow over fairly quickly.'

'Okay...' There was a hint of doubt in her voice. 'If you think so.' She looked at Connor, but he made no further comment. He was watching her, his gaze brooding, and she wondered if he was thinking about the day's events. 'Would you like me to get you some coffee, Connor? You look as though you could do with a cup.'

'Thanks. That would be good.' His gaze travelled to the mass of coppery curls that framed her face, lighting on the beaded clips that held her hair back and then dipping down to the silver necklace at her throat. For a moment she thought he was going to say something more but he stayed silent, and she turned to go into the kitchen. Both men followed her.

'Have you had a bad day?' she asked Connor as she switched on the coffee maker and set out mugs on the island bar. 'You look weary.'

He frowned. 'Let's just say, I've known better. I lost a patient today…a road-accident victim.'

Her green eyes clouded with compassion. 'I'm so sorry.' Despite her ambivalent feelings about him, Alyssa was torn by the tinge of raw emotion she saw on his face. She knew what it felt like to come home after a particularly bad day at the hospital.

Seeing those same feelings echoed in Connor's demeanour made her want to go to him and put her arms around him to offer sympathy and support. But after what had happened on the beach the other day, she had to steel herself to keep some distance between them.

He pressed his lips together briefly. 'We did everything we could, but it was hopeless from the start, really. His injuries were too severe, and he'd lost a lot of blood.'

She nodded, understanding what he was going through. 'You try to tell yourself you've given your best, but it doesn't help when the outcome is bad, does it? That awful sense of loss is always going to be there.' She sent him a quick glance. 'Was it the motorcyclist from the other day? You said he had multiple injuries.'

'No, fortunately he's recovering after surgery. It'll be a long job, but he's on the mend.' He accepted the mug of coffee she offered him and took a slow, satisfying sip. 'It's the same with Alex. He's recovering, but he has a long path ahead of him.'

'Yes, I realised that when I went to see him at lunchtime.' She recalled Alex's mixed feelings, pleasure at having visitors, and frustration with his situation. 'He wants to walk, but the signals from his brain are not getting to his legs properly and so he's finding it very difficult. It may be that the spinal cord is badly bruised and perhaps things will improve with time.'

'We're doing what we can for his family, in the meantime,' Ross said. 'There will be an insurance payout, but until that's finalised we're making sure that they can pay their rent and put food on the table.'

She smiled at him and laid her hand on his in acknowledgement. 'That must be a huge relief for him.'

'It is.' He returned her smile and squeezed her hand. 'It's one less pressure on him, anyway.'

'So how have things gone for you this week?' Connor dragged his gaze from where her hand was engulfed in Ross's larger one, and looked Alyssa in the eyes. 'Have you managed to steer clear of any major casualties?'

'It's been good.' Conscious of his narrow-eyed scrutiny, she carefully extricated her hand. 'I haven't had to do much at all, except to soak up the sun while I've watched the film being made. I'm looking forward to spending a few more weeks doing that.'

'Hmm.' Connor studied her thoughtfully. 'Doesn't it ever bother you, the fact that you have great medical skills at your fingertips and yet you're not using them? You showed your expertise when you worked on Alex. Doesn't it ever occur to you that you're wasting years of expensive medical training by opting out?'

She sucked in a sharp breath. He'd delivered a thrust that had gone directly to her heart. She hadn't been expecting it, and the way he'd said it, in such a straightforward, matter-of-fact way, somehow made it seem all the worse.

'I don't see it that way. I felt I needed a change of direction.' There was a faint quiver in her voice. 'I'm doing what's right for me at the moment.' She shook her head. 'I don't expect you to understand.'

Ross wrapped his arms around her. 'Don't let my brother get to you. He's sometimes very blunt and doesn't realise how he might hit a nerve.' Glaring at Connor, he said in a terse voice, 'You shouldn't judge Alyssa that way. You don't know her well enough.'

'Obviously not.' Connor's gaze darkened as Ross kissed Alyssa lightly on the temple and hugged her close. He straightened up and moved away from the worktop. 'I'm going up to my apartment to take a shower. Enjoy your evening…if you still insist on going. Just take care, and make sure you watch out for any warning signs. You might find you need to stay at the bar until things settle down.'

'I doubt that'll be necessary,' Ross answered. 'We'll be home by ten-thirty at the latest, because we have to get an early start tomorrow. We're shooting the scenes that take place at sunrise.'

Connor acknowledged that with a nod and left the room, but Ross kept his arms around Alyssa for a moment or two longer.

She looked up at him. 'Could he be right? I mean…'

'You worry too much. We get used to these

tropical storms around here.' He smiled and dropped a gentle kiss on her mouth. 'You should try to relax a little.'

She sent him a cautious glance. 'Ross…you know Connor has the wrong idea about you and me, don't you? He thinks we're involved with one another, and it doesn't help when he sees you hold me this way. It's bound to make him think there's something going on.'

Ross sighed. 'Yeah, I know.' He looked into her eyes. 'And there isn't anything between us, is there? Not on your part, right?'

Alyssa frowned. She had to deal with this, once and for all. Ross had to understand the way she felt. 'You know how I feel, don't you? We're friends, Ross…great friends, but that's all. I can't think of you any other way. Besides, after the way my ex treated me, I'm not even going to think of getting involved again. It's just too painful. I'm sorry.'

'I know.' He ran a hand down her bare arm, his expression filled with sympathy and understanding. 'As for Connor, I know he has the wrong idea about you and me, but that annoys me. He's my big brother and he's always looked out for me since I was small, but it's time he realised I can make my own decisions for good or bad.' He laid a finger beneath her chin. 'I can't resist tormenting him a little, just to teach him a lesson. You're a good person and he shouldn't let his prejudices rule him.'

She shook her head. 'Even so, I want you to stop. It isn't helping and I don't like him getting the wrong impression.'

'Okay.' He slowly released her. 'I'm not promising anything, but I'll try.'

They left for the Reef Bar a short time later, and met up with friends in the lounge area where doors had been opened onto a covered terrace to let in the fresh evening air.

The atmosphere was boisterous and happy, with heavy beat music coming from a group of men playing drums, cowbells and whistles, along with a brass section made up of horns, trumpets, trombones and tuba. It was lively and very loud so that Alyssa had almost to shout to make herself heard.

'I'll get you a drink,' Ross said. 'What will you have? They do all sorts of cocktails here.'

She studied the list, written up on a board at the side of the bar. 'Hmm…let me see… Tequila Sunset sounds good…a mix of vodka and Cointreau…and so does Yellow Bird.' That was made from a herbal liqueur called Galliano and added rum. She mulled things over. 'But I think I'll go with Brown Skin Girl.' It was a mix of rum with crème de cocoa, cranberry and orange juice, and when Ross handed it to her it was in a wide-rimmed cocktail glass filled with ice and topped with a cherry.

'Mmm…this is delicious,' she told him, taking a sip. She noticed he wasn't drinking anything alcoholic, probably because he would be driving later. It didn't seem to spoil his fun, though, because he joined in with the general chatter, laughter and dancing, pulling her out onto the wooden dance floor to move to the rhythm of the Caribbean.

They danced and chatted with members of the film crew and cast, and the time passed so quickly that Alyssa was taken by surprise when it was time to leave.

'Do you want to stay on?' Ross asked. 'I could arrange a lift, or a taxi, for you.'

'No, don't do that. I'll go home with you,' she told him, and together they went to say their goodbyes to everyone.

'I've had a wonderful time,' she murmured, as they left the bar a short time later.

'So have I.' He pushed open the side door that led on to the car park, and for the first time that day Alyssa felt the chill of the breeze on her bare arms. She shivered a little, and Ross put his arm around her to warm her. Looking about her, she noticed the branches of a nearby casuarina tree shaking wildly in the breeze, its thin, needle-like leaves tossed about with casual ease.

'It's going to rain,' Ross said, looking at the leaden sky. He frowned. 'Let's get to the car before it starts.'

His car was a sleek silver saloon, and Alyssa

was glad to slip into the passenger seat as his prediction came true. Her bare arms were already wet and within a few seconds the initial individual raindrops had turned into a lashing downpour. She could hear it beating down on the roof of the car.

'Do you think we ought to follow Connor's advice and stay at the bar until the storm passes over?' she asked, looking out of the window at the growing turbulence all around. The wind had become almost violent in nature, and there was a noise, an ominous sound in the background, that she couldn't quite fathom.

Ross frowned. 'That could mean we're stuck here for hours,' he said. 'We're only about twenty minutes' drive away from home, so we could probably make it back before things get too bad.'

'I suppose so.' She wasn't convinced, and she was still worried about that loud, booming sound she could hear, even from within the relatively safe interior of the car. She saw that the Reef's bartenders were beginning to close the doors and draw the shutters over the windows. 'What's that noise I can hear? Do you know?'

'It's probably the sea,' he answered. 'The danger from these tropical storms isn't to do with the wind so much as the sea. It gets whipped up and the waves build up and the water starts to encroach on the land. Any inlets or streams quickly get swollen with flood water.'

'That doesn't sound too good.'

'No. But we're some distance from the ocean here, so we probably don't need to worry too much.'

A thought struck her, and her brows drew together in a frown. 'But we're right next to the sea back at the house. Doesn't that mean Connor's in danger?' The fact that he might be in trouble made her want to rush back right away.

Ross shook his head. 'We're on the leeward side of the island, so we're relatively sheltered there. And the trees and shrubs tend to act as a windbreak. We're on quite a raised plot, too, which is why you can look out over the sea from there. Connor will be all right.'

She was relieved. 'That's something, at least.' She wasn't happy about going on but, then, she wasn't used to life on the island, whereas Ross had lived here most of his life. She'd follow his lead.

He started up the car and they headed out along the road towards the main highway. Alyssa was apprehensive, watching the branches of the trees that lined their route sway dangerously in the wind. Some of the less sturdy ones would lose their branches if things became much worse, she felt sure.

Ross turned the car onto a quiet, rural road. 'This should be the safer option, I think,' he murmured. 'It's less open to crosswinds.'

She nodded, following his logic, but she was cautious about the tall trees that stood like menacing sentinels on either side of the road. The sky was ominously dark, and the trees appeared as black figures against the skyline, their branches dipping and swooping in a frightening way.

There was a sudden creaking and a crashing sound as one of the smaller trees seemed to uproot itself and she stared at it in horror as it started to fall across their path. Ross was quick to take evasive action, turning the steering wheel vigorously and driving towards the opposite side of the road, but Alyssa had the dreadful feeling that it was too late. Her stomach clenched in fear as a massive branch fell across the front of the car, smashing into them. At the same time the car came to a sudden stop as Ross slammed on the brakes.

Alyssa instinctively bent her head and covered her face with her arms as the thick windscreen glass groaned and shattered. Small pieces of laminated glass fell over her, but as the car shuddered to a halt, she gradually came to realise that, apart from some possible bruising from the emergency braking, she was all right. She wasn't hurt. She sat up, brushing blunt fragments of glass from her hair, and turned to look at Ross.

What she saw left her rigid with shock. Some of the tree's branches had speared the windscreen, coming through on the driver's side, and Ross was slumped over the wheel. There was a gash to the side of his head, and even in the darkness she could see that blood was trickling from it down his cheek.

Heart thumping, she felt for a pulse at his wrist. It was beating, an erratic kind of rhythm, but it was there and he was still alive. She sighed with relief, but it was short-lived. What would she do if his condition began to deteriorate? How would she cope?

'Ross, can you hear me? Can you talk to me?'

He mumbled something, and she tried again. 'I need to know if you're hurt anywhere other than your head,' she said slowly. 'Talk to me, Ross.'

Somehow, she was going to have to get them out of this mess, but for now she couldn't think what to do. It wouldn't be wise to move him, because he might have sustained a whiplash injury or worse when the branch had struck him. She flipped on the car's interior light and looked around to see if there was anything she could use to make a neck collar that would prevent him from sustaining any more damage.

In the back seat of the car she saw a newspaper, quickly leaned over to get it and began to roll it with trembling hands into a serviceable, tight wad. There was some tape in the glove compartment, and she used this to secure it around his neck. Then she gently eased him back in the seat so that the headrest supported his head. Blood oozed from his wound and he started to retch.

She searched in her handbag and found some tissues. They weren't much use, but they would help to contain things a bit if he was sick.

She breathed deeply and tried to pull herself together. Foraging in her handbag once more, she found her mobile phone and dialled the emergency services' number, only to discover that there was no signal. Dismayed, she thought through her options. Judging from what had happened to her, the ambulance and rescue services would probably be overrun with calls right now. She'd heard about the nature of these storms and could only imagine the damage that would have been caused to property, especially in the poorer areas.

She sat back in her seat and fought to stem the

tide of panic that ran through her. The front of the car was completely destroyed, rendering the car out of action, even if she'd had the strength to move the tree.

She had never felt so completely alone. On a dark, stormy night she was stranded on a lonely road in the middle of nowhere, in a strange country, and for a second or two she felt a wave of panic wash through her. Her heart was thumping wildly. If only Connor was here. He would know what to do.

Only he wasn't here, and he was way too sensible to ever have risked coming out on a night like this. Would he even know that they were in trouble?

All she could do was to sit things out and wait for the storm to abate. They were off the road, as far as she could see, so they should be safe from any traffic at least. It seemed that when he'd seen what was about to happen, Ross had swerved onto a verge on the opposite side of the road. The tree was a worry, though, a danger to other road users.

'Ross, how are you doing? Are you able to talk to me? Please try to answer me.' Somehow she had to get him to respond.

He mumbled something once more, words that she couldn't make out, but at least it meant he was semi-conscious. He didn't appear to have any other wounds, just the nasty gash on his head.

She didn't know how long she sat there, but lights suddenly dazzled her, coming from straight ahead. Was it another motorist heading towards them? She had to warn the driver about the fallen tree blocking his path. Ought she to stop who-ever it was and ask for help? At least he might help them to get to a hospital.

The other car was still some distance away so she might yet be able to catch the driver's atten-tion. She reached over and switched on the lights, flashing them on and off several times. Then she pushed open the passenger door and tried to step out into the road.

The force of the billowing, gusty wind almost knocked her over and she fought desperately to keep her balance, holding onto the car door.

In the gloom she saw that the other driver had stopped and was getting out of his vehicle.

'What on earth are you doing? Get back inside the car.' It was Connor's voice and she was so stunned to see and hear him that she stayed where she was and stared at him, wide-eyed and open-mouthed.

'In the car,' he said again, taking her by the arm and urging her back inside. Making sure she was securely settled in her seat, he came and sat in the back of the vehicle.

He must have been shocked by what he'd seen as he'd driven towards them, but he steeled himself now to reach forward and examine his brother, quickly assessing the damage.

Alyssa struggled to gain control of herself. Relief had washed over her when she'd seen him, but now the enormity of the situation was bearing down on her. Her heart beat a staccato rhythm. 'He has a head injury,' she told him, 'but he's semi-conscious. I've been trying to talk to him, to keep him awake.'

He nodded. 'We'll have to get him to the hospital. It's not too far from here.'

'I wanted to do that, but I knew, from the size of it, that I wouldn't be able to shift that tree on my own.'

'Of course you couldn't.' He studied her, his expression taut. 'Are you all right? Are you hurt in any way?'

She shook her head. 'I'm fine,' she said.

'Are you sure?' He reached out and touched her cheek as though he would physically check her out. 'You were shaking when I first got here.'

'Really, I'm okay.' She frowned. 'What are you doing here, anyway? How did you know we needed help or where to find us?' That had to be the only reason he was out here on a night like this. He'd come specially to find them.

'When you didn't come home when I expected you I tried to call both of you on your mobiles. I guessed there was no signal, which made me all the more concerned. But I managed to get through to the Reef Bar on a landline, and the bartender told me you had left there almost an hour previously. I was worried.' His expression tightened. 'I didn't like to think what might have happened to you.'

'So you came to find us.' Thank goodness he had cared enough to do that. The brothers might have their differences from time to time, but Connor's loyalty was unshakeable. She frowned. 'You took a big risk coming out here, knowing what conditions were like.'

'I had to find out what had happened. Anyway, I have a solid, four-wheel drive that I keep for times like these. I assumed Ross would have avoided the main highway.'

He looked around. 'Okay, you stay here. I'm going to try to move the tree to make things safer for anyone else who comes this way. Then I need to get Ross out of here.'

'I'm coming with you.' She'd already started to slide out of the car, and when he started to object, she said quickly, 'You'll need help.'

Perhaps he could see from the determined tilt of her chin that there was no point in arguing with her. 'Make sure you keep hold of something at all times,' he said.

They set to work. Between them they attempted to pull the tree from the car, battling all the while against the raging storm. Rain drove into Alyssa, drenching her, and the wind took her breath away.

'Here, give me your hand,' Connor said when he was satisfied the road was clear. 'I'll help you back to the car.' She did as he asked and they huddled together against the driving force of the wind.

'Sit back in the car while I move Ross,' he said, but she shook her head.

'I'll give you a hand. We don't know if he has any other injuries, and we need to be as careful as possible,' she warned him. 'I'll hold the door open for you.'

He pressed his lips together. 'All right… But, as before, make sure you keep hold of the car, or me, at all times.'

'Okay.'

He went around to the driver's side and slowly, carefully, eased Ross over his shoulder in a fireman's lift. Alyssa helped to keep Ross's body from twisting or jerking in any way, and between them they managed to transfer him to the back of Connor's car. Even in the darkness she could see it was a top-spec model. There was no time to dwell on that, though. The gale howled all around them, whipping the branches like a maddened beast. Alyssa's teeth started to chatter.

Connor made sure that his brother was securely fastened into his seat, and covered him with a blanket that he retrieved from the boot of the car. Alyssa went to sit beside Ross, talking to him the whole time, trying to get him to answer her. Connor took off his jacket and draped it over her.

'But you'll need it,' she protested.

He gave her a wry look. 'I think right now you need it more than I do.'

He went around to the boot of the vehicle once more and came back a moment later to hand her a first-aid kit. 'There are dressings in there, and bags in case he's sick.' He frowned. 'He's badly concussed.'

Then he slid into the driver's seat and started

the engine. The car purred into action and a moment or two later heat began to waft around Alyssa as he engaged climate control. It was one small comfort after what they'd been through. Very soon they were on their way to the hospital.

They'd gone a mile or so, and had emerged from the leafy lane to turn on to a road leading to a small settlement area. A creek ran alongside a cluster of wooden houses, and Alyssa guessed it had burst its banks and flooded the area, because the land all around was awash with water. She could see the moon glinting on the surface ripples. Flimsy roofs had been torn off the wooden outhouses, and here and there doors were missing.

She peered through the gloom. Even with such conditions causing havoc all around them, a group of people huddled in the wide, covered entrance to what she guessed was an old, brick schoolhouse. One of them, a man in his thirties, she guessed, started to wave frantically, trying to get them to stop.

Connor carefully drew the vehicle to a halt,

glancing at Ross in the back. 'Are you still with us, Ross?' he asked.

Ross mumbled a reply. His eyes were closed and he seemed oblivious to what was going on. Alyssa had covered the gash on his head but the dressing was soaked with blood.

Connor wound down his window a little. 'What's the problem?' he asked.

'It's my little girl—she was swallowed up by the creek—it swept her away and she nearly drowned. We rescued her, but we can't get her to breathe—she needs to go to hospital. Can you help us?'

Alyssa wondered what the child was doing up at this time of night. Whatever the reason, it was a horrendous situation these people had found themselves in—she doubted that any of them had transport that would withstand the journey to the hospital.

She glanced at Ross, wondering if she dared leave him, because Connor was already climbing out of the vehicle to go and see what he could do to help. 'I'm a doctor,' he told the distraught man. 'I'll see what I can do.'

Now that she focussed more clearly, Alyssa could make out a small figure lying in the covered porch. The child couldn't be much more than five years old, she guessed.

Connor knelt down beside the girl and checked her breathing and her pulse. Then he looked in her mouth for any obstruction and made a finger sweep search. Alyssa guessed he found something because he shook the debris free of his hand and started to press down on her chest, with steady, rhythmic movements.

Alyssa made up her mind what she had to do. Turning to Ross, she said urgently, 'I'm sorry, Ross, but I have to go. I won't be long, but I think Connor might need some help. I promise I'll be back with you in a few minutes.'

Keeping her head down, she struggled through the storm to get to Connor. Hands reached for her, and the small assembly drew her into the relative safety of the archway.

She knelt down beside Connor. 'What can I do?' she asked.

'Take over from me. I'll go and get the oxygen kit from my car.'

'Okay.' She took his place, going on with the CPR, while Connor searched in the boot for his medical kit. The little girl wasn't moving. She was deathly white, her lips taking on a bluish tinge, and Alyssa's heart turned over with dread. How could this happen to such a small, helpless child?

'Can you do anything for her?' the father pleaded. 'She isn't breathing, is she?' His voice broke. 'We were having a birthday celebration. That's why she was up so late. But then she wandered outside...'

Connor returned and straight away checked the little girl's pulse. 'It's very faint, but she's still with us...' He looked down at her frail form. 'Just a little more effort, sweetheart. Breathe for me. Try to fill your lungs, you must breathe.'

He placed the mask over her face and then looked up at the child's father. 'What's her name?'

'Bijou. It means "jewel".'

Connor smiled. 'That's a lovely name.' Then he turned back to the child and said softly, 'Breathe for me, Bijou. You can do it, I know you can.'

Alyssa watched him. He cared so much that this tiny girl should live. He wasn't going to give up on her while there was the remotest chance, and she desperately wanted him to succeed. She was numb inside, scared about what might happen, but she went on with the CPR without interruption as Connor rhythmically squeezed the oxygen bag.

Bijou suddenly spluttered, turning her head to one side and dislodging the mask. She coughed and seemed to choke, and then after a second or two she tried desperately to suck air into her lungs. When she settled once more, Connor held the mask over her nose and mouth. 'That's it. Good girl. Take your time. Breathe in...that's it, nice and deep.'

Alyssa smiled, overcome with joy. 'She's going to be all right.' She glanced up at the parents. 'We must take her to hospital all the same, to make sure everything's as it should be.' There could be some irritant after-effects of having water in her lungs, and the hospital would be the best place to make sure she received the right support.

Connor agreed. 'We can take her, along with one parent. I'm sorry, but I've no room for any more because my brother's injured and I have to take him to hospital. Who will it be?'

'I'll go with her.' The child's mother stepped forward. Her face was drained of colour, etched with the strain of seeing her daughter struggle for life. 'Thank you so much for what you've done. I don't know what to say. I can't thank you enough.'

Bijou's father joined in. 'Yes, yes…a thousand thanks. We owe you so much. Thank you.'

The small crowd of people helped them back to the car. The little girl was very cold but they managed to find a blanket for her, and Alyssa removed her wet dress and carefully wrapped her up warmly before placing her beside her mother in the back of the car.

Both she and Connor checked on Ross. He was

still quiet, sitting with his eyes closed, occasionally retching.

Alyssa was glad of the warmth of the car once more. Connor drove carefully, looking ahead for signs of trouble but keeping on a steady path towards the hospital. It was hard to believe the evening had turned out so badly.

'We're here. Let's get everyone inside.'

Alyssa looked around, startled to find that they were at Coral Cay Hospital already. Her mind had wandered, thinking about Connor's calm, assured actions as he'd battled to save the small child, and how careful he'd been to make sure his brother came to no harm. She didn't like to dwell on either outcome if he hadn't turned up when he had.

He made his report to the on-duty registrar, and Bijou was whisked away to the paediatric ward. The registrar spoke soothingly to the child's mother. 'We'll make sure she's thoroughly warm and then we'll examine her to be certain there's no ongoing damage,' he said. 'She may need a chest X-ray and antibiotics, or possibly even medication to stop any spasm of the airways. That can sometimes happen a few hours after the event, so we'll keep her in for observation.'

Ross was wheeled to a treatment bay, where one of the emergency doctors started to check him over, looking for signs of neurological damage. 'We'll get the wound cleaned up and apply a fresh dressing,' he told Connor. 'He'll probably be glad of some painkillers, too. Leave him with us for a while.'

He looked Connor over and then glanced at Alyssa. 'You both look as though you could do with getting out of those wet clothes. We could find you some fresh scrubs to wear and then maybe you'd like to warm up from the inside. Our cafeteria is still open.'

'That sounds good to me. Hot soup would be just the thing.' Connor sent Alyssa a questioning glance, and she nodded, her mind somewhere else, watching the small girl being wheeled away.

It was beginning to dawn on her how close she had come to seeing a child die. The thought hit her like a hammer blow, leaving a heavy, aching feeling in the pit of her stomach. She felt faint. She didn't know how to handle the emotions that rippled through her like a shock wave.

Connor held out his hand to her. 'I'll show you where you can change,' he murmured. He gave her a sideways glance, a questioning look in his eyes.

She nodded, unable to answer him just then. The events of the night were beginning to crowd in on her and she had an overwhelming feeling that she was about to cry. The responsibility of being a doctor was awesome, and she didn't think she could cope with it for much longer.

He showed her to a room where she could dress in private, and handed her a large, white towel and a set of scrubs.

'Thanks.'

He left her, again with that thoughtful, musing glance, and once she was alone she stared at herself in the mirror that had been fixed to the wall.

She looked a mess. Her dress clung to her, and her hair had reverted to a mass of unruly curls, the way it did whenever it was wet. Connor, on the other hand, had looked as good as ever, with his shirt plastered to his chest and a damp sheen outlining his angular features. He was strong and capable, and she didn't know how she would have managed without him.

She removed her dress and towelled herself dry then put on the hospital scrubs, loose-fitting cotton trousers and a short-sleeved top. As for her hair, she did what she could with the towel and then used the hot-air machine next to the sink to get rid of the worst of the damp.

There was a comb in her handbag, and she ran it through her curls, restoring as much order as was possible. A smear of colour on her full lips made the final touch, and she braced herself to go and meet with Connor once more.

'Are you feeling a bit better?' he asked, and she nodded.

'Yes, thanks.'

'Good. I had some food brought down from the cafeteria. It's all set up in my office. I thought it might be a bit more private in there. You don't feel much like company, do you?'

'No, you're right. I don't.' She tried a smile. 'That was thoughtful of you.'

He led the way to his office, putting an arm around her waist, the flat of his hand splayed out over her rib cage. 'Here we are. Do you want to take a seat on the couch? You might be more comfy there.'

She sat down on the luxurious leather couch, and he brought a tray over to the small table in front of her. A coffee pot and cups had already been set out there, along with cream and sugar, but on the tray there was a small tureen of soup, together with bowls and an assortment of bread rolls. He lifted the lid from the tureen, and the appetising aroma of chicken and vegetables filled the air.

'This will warm you through and through,' he said, ladling the rich mixture into the bowls. Then he came to sit beside her and for a few minutes they sat in silence, appreciating the food and waiting while the hot soup helped to make the chill of the night disappear from their bones.

'You seemed very upset after we treated the

little girl,' he said when she finally laid down her spoon. 'Perhaps the events of the night were beginning to catch up with you. You must have been shocked by what happened, with the tree coming down and everything that followed.'

She nodded. 'I was. You don't realise it so much at the time, but afterwards it comes home to you.'

'And looking after the child was the clincher, perhaps?' He opened up a box from the tray and produced a couple of glazed fruit tarts for dessert, gloriously exotic, with small slivers of strawberries, kumquats and kiwi, topped with raspberries and blueberries.

'I suppose so.' She accepted the tart he offered, but didn't begin to eat. He obviously wanted to know what had happened to suddenly make her become so emotional, and perhaps she owed it to him to tell him the truth after the way he'd risked everything to come and find her and Ross.

'The thing is, I don't seem to deal very well with those kinds of situations any more.' She frowned. 'That's a bad thing for a doctor to say, isn't it?' When he didn't answer, she pressed her lips together briefly and went on, 'I worked in emergency back in the UK, and for a time everything was fine. I was good at my job and people respected me. I always did what I could to make sure I pulled people through and helped them back on their feet.'

She hesitated, lost in thought for a moment or two, and Connor began to pour coffee, sliding a cup across the table towards her. 'Go on, please... you were saying you worked in emergency...'

'Yes. Then, one day I witnessed an accident. I was there when it happened, sitting at a table in an open-air café, watching the traffic go by. A man was at work, up a ladder, painting the window frames of the building next door to the café. His wife and children were sitting at the table next to me, talking to him as he worked, enjoying a light snack. It was a beautiful summer day and they seemed such a lovely, happy family. I think they'd been out on a shopping trip and had come to the café especially to see him. Every now and again he would stop what he was doing to pass a comment or two.'

She thought back to that time and a vivid picture filled her mind, blanking out everything else.

She sipped the coffee and realised that her hand was shaking so badly that Connor reached out to cup her hand in his, holding it steady and keeping the coffee from spilling over. 'It's all right, I have you,' he murmured. 'Are you able to go on?'

She nodded and pulled in a deep breath. 'He was in his early thirties, I think. Perhaps it was because I saw it happen that it made such an impact on me. Usually, in emergency, we see people as they come in to hospital. We treat them, patch them up, and we don't really get deeply involved in their lives and relationships, do we? We can be a little bit impartial.' She frowned. 'Does that sound bad? I mean, we do care, but...'

'I know what you mean,' Connor said. 'We don't know them when we're treating them. It's only afterwards, when they're recovering, that we begin to feel the impact.' He looked into her eyes. 'Did something happen to this man?'

She nodded again, swallowing hard. 'The café

was situated on a bend in the road. All of a sudden a car came around the bend, going way too fast, and mounted the pavement. It crashed into the ladder and took out part of the wall of the building. The young man fell and went through the windscreen.' She closed her eyes briefly.

Connor helped her to put her cup down on the table. 'That must have been awful,' he said quietly.

'Yes, it was.' She clasped her fingers together in her lap. 'The driver escaped with just a broken arm and whiplash, plus a few cuts and bruises. I did what I could for both of them, but the decorator suffered a head wound and arterial bleeding. I managed to stop it and I tried to stabilise him on his journey to hospital. I even thought he might stand a chance…but it turned out that he was bleeding internally, and we couldn't do anything to stop it. The…the damage was too great.' Her eyes filled with tears.

He wrapped his arms around her. 'Here, let me hold you. I think maybe you need to let this all out. Have you never talked to anyone about this before now? I mean, properly talked about it, about how much it upset you? I get the feeling you haven't.'

She shook her head, taking up his invitation and nestling against him, letting the tears slowly trickle down her cheeks. There'd been no one she could talk to, no one who would really understand how she felt. 'No one had any idea what it felt like.'

Her parents had frowned, alarmed to hear about what had happened, but they had soon forgotten about it and moved on. To them, it was a moment of conversation. And James… James hadn't been able to understand why she wasn't able to shake off the images. 'Put it behind you,' he'd said. 'You deal with injured people every day. You'll get over it.'

It was expected of her that she would carry on. And she had, for a long time, until one day it had all become too much for her. There had been too many critically ill patients and she had found it more and more difficult to go on. Soon after that, Ross had stepped into her life.

Connor comforted her, his hand gently stroking her back, her arm, as she wept into his shirt. She felt secure in his embrace, as though he was sheltering her from the world. He didn't say anything but waited patiently until she became still, until she managed to pull herself together and started to dash the wetness from her eyes.

'I'm sorry,' she said, straightening up. She shouldn't be burdening him with her problems. Why would he care? 'I know I should be stronger. I despise myself for being so weak.'

'You shouldn't worry about that. Take your time. Take a few deep breaths and you'll start to feel better.'

She nodded, sitting up and sweeping her fingers across her cheeks to clear away any remaining dampness. Then there was a knock at the door of the office and the registrar came in. Alyssa picked up her coffee cup, holding it in both hands to enjoy the warmth, and she sat with her head down, absorbed in her own thoughts. She didn't want to face anyone right now.

'Your brother is coming round,' the registrar

told Connor. He smiled. 'I thought you'd like to know. He's going to be okay.'

'That's great news. Thanks. I'll be along to see him in a minute.'

'Okay.' The registrar left the room, and Connor turned to face her once more.

'I'm glad Ross is recovering,' she said.

'So am I.' He pushed the fruit tart towards her. 'Eat it,' he said. 'They're delicious. I think you need something tasty and exotic right now.'

'They look wonderful, almost too good to eat, don't they?' She looked up at him, suddenly concerned. 'I shouldn't have loaded all my troubles onto you. I'm sorry about that. And anyway, you have other things on your mind. I know he's going to be okay, but even so Ross needs...'

'It sounds as though he's going to be absolutely fine. I expect they'll keep him under observation for a few hours, maybe overnight, and then let him go.' He dipped a spoon into his tart and tasted the fruit. 'Mmm...fantastic.' She had the feeling he was eating in order to encourage her to do the same.

She followed his cue and started to eat. When they had both finished, he stood up and said, 'I'm going to see how my brother is doing. Do you want to stay here for a while and relax with another cup of coffee?'

'No, thank you. That was really good, but I'm full up now. I'll go with you.'

'Okay.'

They left the room together. Connor made no mention of what had gone before, and she couldn't help wondering what he thought about what she'd said. She wished she'd never given in to her feelings that way. How could she represent her profession when she was emotionally vulnerable and clearly unfit to practise? He must think she was weak and not fit to be a doctor. Wouldn't he have even more reason for doubting her now?

CHAPTER FIVE

'HAVE I called at a bad time? It sounds as though you're a bit breathless, or in a hurry, maybe? Are you getting ready for work?' On the other end of the line, Carys was keen to know what Alyssa was up to, and Alyssa paused for a moment, peering into her wardrobe and taking stock of the situation.

'I'm trying to decide what I should wear for a trip into the mangrove swamps.'

'The mangroves?' Her cousin was intrigued. 'That sounds interesting. What's that all about? Anyway, I'd have thought jeans and a light top would do the trick.'

'Yes, you're probably right.' Alyssa reached into the wardrobe and drew out a pair of white jeans and held them in front of her while she looked in the mirror. 'We're filming there later today, and I need to look okay because…guess what…' She paused for effect. 'I'm going to be on film! Can you believe it? I've been roped in as one of the extras.'

'Wow! And here I was worrying they were working you too hard!'

Alyssa laughed. 'Of course I'll be there in my medical capacity, too. But with any luck everyone will be fine and I'll be able to sit back and enjoy the ride.'

'It sounds great. I'd love to be there with you…' Her voice sounded wistful. 'Maybe we could meet up one weekend? I could come over and visit you, if you like.'

'Oh, Carys, that would be great. How about next weekend?' She chatted with Carys for a little longer and then hurried to get ready for the day ahead. The sun was out in its full glory this morning, and the sky was a tranquil blue. It was all so different from a couple of days ago when the storm had wreaked havoc over the island.

Since filming had been stopped for a couple of days, she'd been out with the teams that had been

hastily set up to help clear up after the devasta-
tion, and at times she'd found herself working
alongside Connor, when he'd been able to grab
a few hours away from work.

Today, though, everything was serene as usual.
The palm trees swayed gently in the breeze, and
bordering the beach everything was rich with vibrant life. From the open doors of her bedroom
Alyssa could see the pretty pink flowers of the
oleander, and on the veranda itself there was a
terracotta pot filled with the flamboyant orange
and yellow blooms of poinciana. Just looking at
them made her feel cheerful.

Strangely, since that evening when Connor had
held her in his arms, she'd felt an odd sense of
release. She didn't understand it at all. But it was
definitely there, this lightening of spirit.

'Are you about ready to be off, then?' Ross
came into the kitchen as she was doing a last-
minute bit of tidying up. He'd been staying with
his brother in the apartment upstairs for the last
couple of days, as Connor insisted on keeping an
eye on him while he was recovering from con-

cussion. 'I wish I was coming with you as we planned, but I suppose Connor's right—the company's insurance people would have all sorts of problems with that.'

'I think it's probably best if you stay at home and rest up for a few days more,' Alyssa told him. 'You certainly look better today than you have done these last couple of days.' Apart from a dressing on his head wound, he seemed to be in reasonably good shape. He'd had an ongoing headache since the accident and some slightly blurred vision, but he'd finished taking painkillers now, and that was hopefully a good sign.

'I'd still rather I was going with you on this trip. I hate sitting back and leaving everything to other people.'

'That's because you simply don't know how to delegate,' she said with a laugh. 'Dan *is* the director, you know. You have to let him handle things.'

'Hmmph. Maybe.' He was in a grumpy mood, and that wasn't like him at all.

She patted his hand. 'Take some time out to lie back in the hammock,' she told him, pointing to the canvas that was strung up outside between two palm trees. 'It'll do you the world of good.'

'Yeah, right. Anyway, I'm sorry I won't be able to take you to meet up with the cast and crew— Connor has a day off, though, and he said he'll take you, so there won't be any need for you to call a taxi.'

'Yes, he mentioned it to me last night,' she said as she stacked crockery into the dishwasher. She'd been surprised by his offer. 'I really didn't want to put him out—he leads such a busy life and I'd have thought he'd welcome the chance to stay home and do nothing for a change. He even had to go out somewhere this morning. I heard his car start up as I was thinking about getting out of bed.'

Ross nodded. 'He went to see my father. He rang up this morning, complaining of stomach pains, and said he didn't want to call his own doctor.'

She frowned. 'I'm sorry to hear that. Do you think it's something serious?'

He shook his head. 'The beginnings of an ulcer,

probably. I expect Connor will give him some tablets. I don't think it helps that my father's constantly at odds with our stepmother—his second wife. She's turned out to be a feisty individual. But, then, his judgement was never very good where women are concerned. He had an affair while he was married to our mother—not a great move, because she divorced him after she found out.' He was quiet for a moment or two, thinking about that. 'We were still quite young when it happened...I think I was about eleven.'

He pulled a face. 'So we became part of a divided family, going from one parent to the other throughout the year. And, of course, after the divorce my father became very attractive to other women who liked the idea of his wealth and the lifestyle it could bring them. I was upset, I remember. I wanted my parents to stay together, and I wanted to protect my mother from being hurt, but I didn't know how. So I poured out my worries to my big brother, and he tried to find ways to make me feel better...when all the time he must have been going through it, too.'

She tried to imagine how Connor must have felt, being torn by the disruption to family life and suddenly worrying about his little brother's well-being. She frowned. 'I can't begin to guess what that must have been like. It must have been so difficult for both of you.'

No wonder Connor was so protective of his brother even now. Back then, being some three years older than Ross, he must have taken it upon himself to shield him from any upsets that might come along. Her heart went out to those young boys struggling to come to terms with the break-up of their family.

'Yeah.' Ross absently massaged his brow with his fingers. 'It was hard when we were young, but that's all in the past now.'

'Is it?' She wasn't so sure about that. 'These things probably leave scars of some sort or another.'

'Well, you could be right. I suppose it was bound to leave some kind of legacy, and we were both at an impressionable age. That must be the reason Connor avoids getting deeply involved with anyone. If things start getting too close for comfort, he tends to bail out. And according to him I go after all the wrong kinds of women.' He made a faint smile.

'He's probably right—I've had a few near misses over the years. I tend to be too trusting, I suspect, and then I realise too late that some women are wowed by the prospect of being with a film producer. I'm just me, but they see me as something else.' He sighed. 'I guess all the up-heaval in our lives was bound to affect us in some way.'

She thought about that when Ross left a few minutes later. It wasn't really a surprise to learn that Connor was reluctant to get involved in rela-tionships in any meaningful way. There had been rumours amongst the cast and crew and peo-ple she'd spoken to at the hospital about women who'd loved and lost him. They'd been keen for something more to develop out of the relation-ship with Connor, but in each case apparently he'd chosen that time to gently engineer a part-ing of the ways.

But she didn't want to dwell on any of that right now. Thinking about Connor only left her confused and distracted. So, instead, she carried on with her chores, wiping down the work surfaces and making sure that everything was spick and span.

Connor arrived back at the house a few minutes later as she was watering the houseplants.

'Is everything all right?' she asked, checking the soil around the base of a fern. He looked ready for the day, dressed in casual clothes, dark trousers and a crisp linen shirt that was open at the neck. He glowed with health, and his keys dangled from his fingers as though he was ready to be on the move again. He was full of vibrant energy, and she resisted an urge to put her arms around him and slow him down. 'Ross told me your father wasn't well…he said he thought it might be a stomach ulcer.'

He nodded. 'I think he'll be okay. At least he seems to be feeling much better now. I gave him some tablets and told him I would speak to his doctor to arrange for tests to be done. There could be a bacterial cause, but he's suffered from ulcers before, and I don't think the atmosphere at home helps. I expect Ross told you about that?'

'A little.' She put away the watering can and turned to face him properly. 'It sounds as though your father and stepmother have a fairly volatile relationship.'

He shrugged. 'Well, you know what they say… he made his bed, now he has to lie in it.'

She frowned. 'You don't seem particularly sympathetic.' Maybe that wasn't altogether unexpected, given the circumstances. 'Ross mentioned that you went through quite a bit of upheaval when your parents split up.'

'Yes, we did, but these things happen. You learn to be philosophical about it in the end. Anyway, I expect they're happy enough. Some people enjoy living life on the edge.'

'Hmm. That wouldn't do for me.' She wondered how much of what he said was bravado. After all, that fourteen-year-old boy, shielding his brother from upset, was very much still part of the man.

'Or me.' He looked around and saw her bag on the table. 'So, are you about ready to leave?'

'I am.' She smiled at him. 'I'm looking forward to this trip. Though I do have a few misgivings. I hope we don't…' She frowned as a sudden thought struck her. 'I mean…we're not likely to come across any nasty creatures, are we? Like crocodiles, maybe? I'm not sure quite how I'd cope with them.'

He laughed. 'No, nothing like that. You'll be quite safe. It's really very tame out there. You might see a few crabs scuttling about in the water, but that's about as dangerous as it gets.' He studied her thoughtfully. 'How are you on the water? Do you think you'll get on all right in a kayak?'

She pondered on that for a moment or two. 'Um…actually, I don't know… I imagine I'll be okay. I've been in a rowboat before, and I can swim, if that's what you're asking.'

He smiled. 'I don't think swimming will be necessary. If by some remote chance you manage to overturn the boat, you'll be able to stand up in the water. It's not very deep.'

'Hmm. That's all right, then.' Her shoulders relaxed as relief washed over her. 'But I was hoping I wouldn't be on my own. These are two-man boats we'll be using, aren't they?' She walked with him to the door.

'That's right. But you'll be with me, so you shouldn't have any problems.'

Her eyes widened. 'You mean…you're coming along on the trip?' Her pulse leapt in response to the unexpected news. 'I didn't realise—I thought you were simply taking me to the meeting point.'

'Oh, no. I'm definitely along for the ride.' His gaze meshed with hers. 'I wouldn't miss out on the opportunity to spend the day with you, would I?'

Warm colour flushed her cheeks. He wanted to be with her?

'And besides,' he went on, 'as one of the partners in the company I've always thought it a good idea to see how things are going with the filming. I need to take an interest and have some say in what goes on.'

Her jaw dropped. 'You're a partner? I didn't know. Ross never said...'

'Did he not? Ah, well...' He opened the passenger door of his car and waited for her to be comfortably seated. 'I helped to set up the company with Ross some years back, but I'm more of a silent partner, so to speak. I'm so busy at the hospital that I don't have time for anything more.'

'I wondered how it was that you came to see the filming whenever you had the chance.' She looked at him as though she was seeing him for the first time. 'What was it that made you get into film production? It's a long way from medicine.'

'True.' He gave it some thought as he started up the car. 'We've always been interested in films—as boys we went to see all the latest blockbusters, and Ross had a knack for seeing how scenes were set up or how things could have been done better. For myself, I thought there was a brilliant opportunity for basing production on these islands. There's a whole lot of glamour and excitement here, all the things that filmgoers want to enjoy.'

'It's not everyone who has the money to contemplate starting such an enterprise. Were you just fortunate that way?'

'I guess so.' He drove along the coast road for a while, so that the vista of the deep blue ocean washing up onto an unbroken stretch of white sand stayed with them along the way. 'My grandfather made a good deal of money from exporting fruit, and he set up a trust fund for us. My father runs a financial consultancy business, and I learned from him how to invest any money I managed to save.' His mouth curved. 'I did pretty well out of it, all things considered.'

'So it seems.' Her eyes were wide with admiration. He'd done more than well. 'I suppose Ross must have done much the same.'

'Yes, he did.' Connor sent her a brief, sideways look. 'Where is he, anyway? I thought he would have been around to see you off.'

'He was. He came down to the apartment for a while, but then he took himself off back upstairs. I think he's feeling a little out of sorts.'

'Poor Ross.' His mouth made a crooked line. 'He hates it when I get to spend time with you.'

'No…no, it isn't that.' She shook her head to emphasise the point. 'He just hates to be away from the filming.'

'Sure he does. He'll get over it soon enough.' Connor was still smiling as he turned the car onto the main highway.

Alyssa sank back in her seat, deep in thought, contemplating the day ahead. Was it true, what he'd said earlier? Was that really why Connor had decided to come along today, because he wanted to be with her? After the way she'd opened up to him the other evening about her failures as a doctor, she hadn't expected him to be at all interested in her. After all, how could he have any respect for her when she didn't respect herself? But now…despite her misgivings about getting involved with him, she couldn't deny that the idea of spending time with him made her insides tingle.

Still, doubt crept in once more. Ever since her ex-boyfriend had let her down and proved untrustworthy, she'd had a problem taking things at face value. Was it actually the company business Connor was most concerned with today? And his reaction to Ross's grumpiness had been a little strange, too. Was he simply taking the opportunity to keep them apart whenever possible? It was all very puzzling.

'Here we are. This is the meeting point,' Connor murmured a few minutes later, and she quickly brought her attention back to the present. They had arrived at a coastal stretch of the island, where a brackish creek flowed into the sea, and people were already beginning to gather by the water's edge. Sliding out of the car, Alyssa went with Connor to join them.

All around everything was green, rich with lush vegetation, and an overhang of densely populated, leafy trees countered the heat of the sun.

They exchanged greetings with everyone who was taking part in the filming, relaxing for a while ahead of the day's events. Then the director stepped forward and spoke to them all for a few minutes, cast and extras, about the course the filming was to take. Dan was a well-built man, florid and exuberant, with brown hair that had been bleached by the sun.

'Okay folks, listen up,' he said. 'You'll be going through the mangrove swamps at a leisurely pace. Try to forget that the camera is on you. You need to be as natural as possible. Take in the scenery all around you as if you're on a pleasure trip. Our leading man will be trying to blend in like one of the tourists, and his major activity won't start until we reach the cave system, so you've no need to be anticipating anything untoward. Is that all clear?'

He looked around, and everyone nodded. 'Good. We'll be heading for the landing point— just follow the lead kayak and ignore the cameras. From there you'll take the boardwalk to the cavern system and the beach, and that's where your part ends. You'll have lunch there. It's all laid on.'

A small cheer went up. 'I hope you've provided something for us to drink,' one bright spark piped up. 'Something of the alcoholic variety would be good.' There were a few more cheers in support.

'Yes, yes, it's all arranged. Along with a bus to take you home again.' Dan clapped his hands together. 'Okay, shall we get on? Time's wasting, and the light's perfect right now. I don't want to lose it.'

Alyssa gazed around her. The mangrove swamp was a truly magnificent sight. Huge trees seemed to walk on the water, their gnarled, tangled roots above the surface and below. Everything was verdant, bustling with life, and through the canopy the sun glinted down on the salt creek.

Connor helped her into their kayak. They were seated one behind the other, with Alyssa at the back, and slowly they edged out into the water, dipping their paddles in unison.

As they moved deeper into the swamp, she was overwhelmed by the serenity of the place. 'It's beautiful here, so peaceful,' she murmured. 'I wasn't expecting that, but it's perfect.' Birds called to one another, darting from tree to tree or gliding leisurely on the wind currents. And when she looked into the forest on either side she saw glimpses of broad-leaved ferns and, here and there, flowers, delicate, beautiful blooms in bright colours. 'They're orchids, aren't they?' she said quietly, her voice full of awe.

'Yes, that's right.' Connor stowed his paddle for a while, allowing them to drift and take in their surroundings, and Alyssa followed his example. 'They grow wild out here,' he said, 'in small pockets in the trunks of the trees or in crevices in the rocks.'

'Somehow I didn't imagine there would be flowers. It's all so lovely, it's breathtaking.'

Connor smiled. 'I thought you'd like it here. It's something we have in common, don't we...a love of nature? Ross and I often came here when we were teenagers, kayaking through the lagoons. I really appreciated it when we moved from Florida and came to live here. I loved everything about the islands. There's so much variety.'

They paddled idly through the water, passing by billowing seagrass and oyster beds, where molluscs had fastened themselves to the underwater tree roots.

They chuckled as a sandpiper teetered along

the bank, in his distinctive wobbling gait, his tail bobbing up and down while he searched for titbits with his orange, pointed bill. And a few minutes later they were startled by the sudden loud call of a green heron that came to settle on the opposite bank.

'That's a bonus for us,' Connor said softly. 'You don't usually see them in the daytime, unless they're hungry or feeding their young.'

Once again they stopped paddling and remained still for a while, following the bird's movements as it picked out insects one by one and then dropped them in the water to attract any passing fish. Then, as soon as he spied his prey, he swooped, triumphant.

Soon, perhaps too soon, Alyssa thought, they reached the landing point, and tied up the kayak, stepping out onto the wooden boardwalk. On either side of them the mangrove forest became a thick, green wall of leaves and branches.

Connor put his arm around her. 'I'm glad you agreed to come along today,' he said quietly. 'I wasn't sure, after the night of the storm, whether you'd still be up for it. Those winds can be scary and they leave a wide trail of damage behind them, one way and another.'

'With people, as well as property, you mean?' She tried not to think about that arm that circled her shoulders and protected her from any stray, encroaching branch as they walked along. 'I was just so glad you came to find us that night. I don't know what I'd have done without you.'

'You'd have found a way to get him to hospital, even if it meant waiting for the next driver to come along. I was fortunate in that I found you first.'

'Yes.' She smiled up at him. 'Thank you for what you did, anyway. I was so impressed by the way you saved that little girl.'

'Ah…that was a joint operation, I think. And by all accounts, she's doing well now.'

'I'm glad about that.' She frowned. 'But what will happen about all the damage to their village? They looked like poor people, so even though things have been cleared up, it might be difficult for them to get the repairs started. I heard of

other villages, too, where there were a few slight
injuries and property was wrecked.'

'Yes, that's true. A number of settlements were
hit, and people need help, but we've organised
workers to go on with the clearing-up process.'
He hugged her briefly. 'I thought it was great
how you pitched in to help. Anyway, at the end
of filming we'll give a gala dinner and invite
people to donate to the fund we're setting up to
help with rebuilding.'

She looked at him with renewed respect. 'By
"we" you mean you and Ross?'

He nodded. 'We couldn't just stand by and do
nothing.'

'No. I think it's great, what you're proposing.'

They walked along the pathway to a sheltered
area of the rock-strewn beach, where the cast
and crew were assembling for a picnic lunch.
To Alyssa's surprise, someone had set up a gas-
fired barbecue beneath the palm trees and a chef
dressed in traditional white jacket and dark trousers was there, already busy preparing food. The
cameraman turned his attention to the inlets and

caves some distance away where the film action was taking place.

Connor found a patch of smooth, white sand a little apart from the crowd, shaded by the branches of a tropical sea grape tree. He sat down, reaching for her hand and pulled her down beside him. The fruits of the tree hung down in clusters above them, purplish-red in colour, as though inviting someone to pick and eat them.

'Mmm…something smells good.' Alyssa's mouth was beginning to water as the appetising aroma of chicken and barbecue ribs filled the air. 'I was expecting something like sandwiches, definitely not hot food.'

'We aim to please.' Connor smiled, and just then a couple of catering staff came around with plates, inviting people to help themselves.

Alyssa was handed a plate and Connor helped her to pick out a selection of crab cakes, served with tangy zucchini and cucumber coleslaw, along with smoked chicken wings and conch fritters. These were served with a spicy dipping sauce, and there was rice and salad to complete the dish.

A table had been set up in the shade of a cavern, where wine bottles were chilling on a bed of ice, and Connor went to fill two glasses with sparkling white wine. He came and sat beside her once more and she realised he'd brought the bottle with him, along with a bucket of ice.

'I think,' Alyssa murmured, after a while, leaning back against a sun-warmed rock, 'this is what I came here for—to the Bahamas, I mean… Sun, sand and sea, and the most delicious food ever.' There had been a wonderful selection of fruit for dessert, a perfect accompaniment to the meal. 'I sometimes think I must have died and gone to heaven.'

Connor laughed. 'Heaven here on earth, perhaps,' he murmured, filling up her glass once more. 'You might as well relax, because we're free for the rest of the afternoon, as the man said.'

She nodded dreamily as she sipped her wine. 'I will. You don't need to encourage me. I can't think of anything I'd rather be doing.'

'You can't?' He moved closer, his hand coming to rest on the soft curve of her hip, and she cautiously set her glass down on a nearby flat rock.

'Connor, I…'

'Maybe I could help you with a few ideas.' He dropped a kiss onto her unsuspecting lips and murmured softly, 'Mmm…you taste of spice and summer fruit…pineapple, I think, and plump, juicy peaches, luscious…just like you.'

She gazed up at him, eyes widening, her lips parting in startled awareness after that dreamy, soft-as-thistledown kiss, while her whole body had begun to fizz with heightened expectation. He'd kissed her just once, and to her shame she wanted more. She wanted to feel his lips on hers all over again and his hands to stroke along the length of her body.

'I…uh…'

'You…uh…need me to show you how to let go of your worries and enjoy being cosseted, don't you?' he said with a smile. 'I can do that, Alyssa. I can make you feel good about yourself. Let me show you…'

He kissed her again, slowly, thoroughly, his hand splayed out over her rib cage, warm, tender, inviting her to lean into the protective curve of his body. And she was sorely tempted. More than anything, she wanted to feel his long body next to hers, to have him hold her and to have him transport her to some magical, sensational world where nothing mattered but the two of them and their slow, sweet exploration of each other.

But something in her resisted, some faint vestige of self-preservation managed to rise above his sensual onslaught. So, instead, she shifted in his arms and even before she pressed the flat of her hand against his rib cage, he had come to realise that all wasn't well.

'What's wrong, Alyssa?' he murmured. His cheek brushed hers, teasing her with his closeness, his lips so near, yet so far, and to her dismay she felt her resistance crumbling at the first hurdle.

'Connor, I…uh…I don't think this is a good idea.'

'Are you sure about that?' he demurred softly.

'That's a great shame because, you know, I'd really like to kiss you again.' His head lowered, his mouth coming dangerously close to hers. 'Why don't you want me to kiss you?'

She made a soft groan. 'I do…but I can't let it happen. I can't get involved. Besides, there are way too many people around. It wouldn't be right. It wouldn't feel right.'

'Should we talk about conflicting signals here?' He gave her a rueful smile. 'Anyway, nobody's taking any notice of us. We're in the shade, away from where all the action is. And they'll be gone soon. The bus will be taking them back in a few minutes.'

'Won't we be on that bus with them?'

He shook his head. 'I've a boat waiting to take us back to the meeting point. I thought you might like to spend some more time here. Was I wrong about that?'

She shook her head. 'No, I love it here.'

'But you don't want to be here with me, is that it?' His features darkened, something bleak flick-

ering in the depths of his eyes. 'Are you still han-
kering after my brother?'

'No, you have it all wrong, Connor. You don't
understand.'

'No, I don't.' He sat up and wrapped his arms
around his knees. 'Perhaps you should explain
it to me.'

She pulled in a deep breath. 'You said I was
giving conflicting signals, and perhaps you were
right about that. I like being with you, I can't
deny it. But you have to know, one of the reasons
I came to the island was because I was in a relationship with someone and it all went wrong.' She
swallowed. 'I thought we had something going
for us, but it fell apart, and in the end I felt I
needed to get away from my ex. He hurt me,
and I don't think I'm ready for the dating scene
again.'

'I'm sorry he hurt you,' he said softly. 'But it
doesn't have to be like that with us. I'm not looking for anything heavy. I told you once before, I
don't want commitment, Alyssa, but you and I
could have fun together. What would be wrong

in that? I like being with you. You're gentle, kind, fun to be with…intelligent… I look forward to seeing you, and whenever I'm with you I want to hold you close and cover you with kisses. Is that so wrong? I get the feeling you like being with me, too.'

'I do. But when it comes down to it, you're talking about sex,' she said in a flat voice. She shook her head. 'I don't go in for meaningless relationships, Connor. I don't sleep around, and I couldn't accept the kind of situation you're suggesting. Besides, maybe things start off that way, leisurely, friendly, no strings attached, but sooner or later, more often than not, the situation begins to change, and someone gets hurt.'

'Like you and your ex?' His glance skimmed over her, tracing a line over her taut features. 'Do you want to tell me what happened?'

She moved her shoulders in an awkward gesture. 'We were together for a couple of years.' She sucked air into her lungs. 'It started off as a mutual friendship and grew into something more as time went by. But then I found I was working

more and more hours in A and E as I special-
ised, while he was left with time on his hands.
He worked at the hospital, doing research, and
his was more or less a nine to five kind of job. I
think he grew tired of waiting for me to finish
my shifts, and sometimes, when we had something planned, I had to let him down because I
couldn't leave my patients in the lurch.'

She frowned. 'I think we might have made a go
of things, all the same, but then I started to suffer
from burnout. I needed someone to talk to, but
suddenly he wasn't there for me. He didn't seem
to understand. And for my part I began to wonder what kind of man he was if I couldn't count
on his support when I needed him.'

'So you broke up with him?'

Her mouth turned down at the corners. 'Not
then, not right away. We talked things through
and decided to try to put things right…only perhaps I was trying a little bit harder than he was.
I went over to his flat early one day, planning to
surprise him with a special dinner for his birthday and tickets to a concert…but I found he was

already celebrating, with a girl from his research department.'

He sucked air into his lungs. 'I'm sorry. That must have come as a killer blow.' His eyes had darkened, his gaze moving over her.

'Yes, it was.' She lifted her chin. 'I suppose you imagine that's par for the course, the kind of thing that happens sooner or later when two people get together.'

He shook his head. 'I'm thinking the man was a fool for playing around when he could have you as his girlfriend.'

She pulled a face. 'Perhaps, deep down, he didn't believe in commitment. Like you.'

'Ouch!' He winced. 'I suppose I deserved that. But the truth is, up to now I've never met any-one that I wanted to commit to. It's not much of a defence, I know.'

He looked so deflated that she couldn't help but smile. 'Shall we just agree to enjoy the rest of the time we have here on the beach? There's more wine in the bottle—I notice you haven't been drinking much—and then I'll look forward to a ride in that boat you said you have waiting.' She frowned as a thought crossed her mind. 'It isn't a rowboat, is it? I really don't fancy paddling my way home along the coast, not after all that delicious food and wine.'

'Oh, it definitely isn't a rowing boat,' he said with a chuckle. 'It has a motor, and a cabin with a galley…as well as all the mod cons that a girl like you might like.'

'I guess that's all right, then. Everything for a girl like me…' What kind of girl did he think she was? She gave him a teasing smile. 'You seem to know me pretty well—but, then, you must have had me more or less sussed out when we first met and you decided I was after Ross for my own mercenary reasons.'

'Ah, but that was way back…an age ago,' he protested, his brows lifting. 'Are you going to keep on holding that against me?'

'Oh, yes,' she said, a glimmer in her green eyes. 'You're definitely not off the hook, by a long way.'

He held a hand to his chest as though she'd

wounded him deeply, and she smiled and sipped the wine he poured for her.

The moment had passed when he would have held her close and kissed her, and she mourned its passing. But it was for the best that she'd held him at bay, wasn't it? It didn't feel too good right now, but she'd get over it soon enough. She hoped.

CHAPTER SIX

'THAT'S a really nasty sunburn you have, Ryan.' Alyssa examined the cameraman's back and shoulders, and frowned. 'How did you manage to get yourself into such a state? Your skin is very red and it's peeling, so there's a risk of infection if it's not treated.'

Ryan winced. 'I was stupid, I know. I didn't think a couple of hours out in the sun without my shirt would hurt. Only we stayed on the beach longer than I expected, and I fell asleep on my front while the others were messing about in the sea.' He moved his hands in a helpless gesture. 'I never knew sunburn could hurt so much. I've been feeling really light-headed and sick.'

'Second-degree burns can be very painful.' She went over to the sink and rinsed a cloth with cold water, giving it to him to hold over his forehead.

'That should cool you down a bit and help take away the sick feeling.'

She checked her medicine cupboard for silver sulfadiazine ointment and used the sterile applicator to spread a thick layer of the cream over the damaged skin. 'This is an antibiotic ointment, to prevent infection,' she told him. 'You'll need to come in every day for the next two or three days so that I can treat you. But I'll put a dressing on the shoulder for you, in the meantime… that's looks to be the worst bit of all.'

'Thanks, Alyssa. You're a gem. It's beginning to feel easier already.'

She smiled. 'It's the coolness, I expect. It's very soothing, but you can help yourself by drinking plenty of fluids—not alcohol but lots of water, juices and so on, over the next day or so to prevent dehydration. And make sure you wear a shirt at all times to keep the area covered.'

'Okay. Thanks again.' He left a few minutes later, clutching a prescription for ibuprofen, to help him deal with the pain.

'Another satisfied customer?' Connor put his

head round the door of her makeshift surgery as she was washing her hands at the sink. The company had provided a mobile unit for her, complete with desk, couch and everything that she would need.

'I hope so. He had a nasty sunburn.'

'It must have been serious if you were using that,' he said, watching her replace the lid on the tub of ointment. 'The natives around here use something natural…gamalamee.'

She sent him a puzzled look. 'I can't say I've ever heard of it.'

'No? It's a bush medicine—the bark of the gumbo limbo tree, or gamalamee, as they call it hereabouts, cut into strips and boiled. When it's cool, they place the strips on the burn to soothe the skin and help it heal.' He smiled. 'It's sometimes known as the tourist tree.'

'Really?' She lifted a brow. 'Why's that?'

'Because the red bark peels, just like the skin of the unfortunate tourists.'

She chuckled. 'I can never be sure whether or not you're teasing me,' she said.

'Not at all. It's quite true. They say it helps a lot with sunburn.' He peered inside her fridge and lifted out a jug of orange juice. 'Is it okay if I help myself?'

'Of course. Glasses are in the cupboard on the wall.'

'Thanks.' He was still smiling as he poured juice for himself and offered a glass to Alyssa. 'It's also true that it's one of the main ingredients in a bush tea called Twenty-One-Gun Salute.' His eyes took on a devilish gleam. 'It's said to be a great aphrodisiac.'

'Hmm. I think maybe we'd best not go there,' she said with a laugh.

'Perhaps you're right. Anyway, you look cool and fresh,' he said, looking her over as she accepted the cold drink. She was wearing a short-sleeved blouse and a loose-fitting skirt that floated lightly around her legs as she walked. 'It's in the high eighties out there.'

'So you've come in here to escape the heat?'

He nodded, taking a long swig from his glass. 'It's my lunch break. I had to go and visit my father to see how he was doing, and this place was on my way back to the hospital, so I thought I'd stop by and see how you were doing.'

'Everything's going fairly well here, up to now, I think. How's your father doing?'

'He's fine. The tests showed some ulceration, nothing more serious than that, and he has medication to clear it up.' He studied her. 'So what's new here?'

She tasted the refreshing juice and took a long swallow. 'Ross is back on site—he looks fit and well, so it seems he's completely over the injury to his head. He's so much back on form that he's getting in Dan's way, I think.'

He chuckled. 'Is he?'

She nodded, giving a faint smile. 'He was talking to Dan about needing to find a stand-in for Alex. There's a water-skiing stunt coming up and they need to get it sorted quickly. Anyway, he told Dan he wants to do the stunt himself.'

He frowned. 'So soon after a head injury? That's definitely not on.'

'Well, everyone seems to think Dan will agree

to it. That's the talk around here today. The thing with this job is that people tend to drop in here and I get to hear all the gossip. They confide all their niggling worries and problems in me.'

'Well, I can see why they might want to do that. I notice that Ross, in particular, calls in on you fairly often.'

'And how would you know that?'

'As you say, people gossip. They know that he's besotted with you. I only have to walk on the set and people are ready to help me catch up on the news.'

She absorbed that while he finished his drink and glanced at his watch. 'Perhaps I should be getting back—' He broke off as someone knocked on the door, and then Ross came in, supporting one of the stagehands, who appeared to be ill. He was also limping badly, and leaning on Ross as best he could.

'Bring him over to the couch,' Alyssa said quickly. She recognised the young man as one of the workers who had helped with the clean-up after the storm a few days ago. She'd stood alongside him in the flooded area of a small settlement and piled debris onto a waiting truck.

'What's wrong, Lewis?' she asked. 'How can I help?'

'It's my foot,' he said, struggling for breath. 'The pain is really bad.' He was shivering, too, and looked as though he might pass out at any moment. This couldn't simply be a problem with his foot, she realised. The man was sick.

'Shall I take off his shoe and sock?' Ross asked, when the man was settled on the couch. She nodded.

'Please. I need to take a look.' She put on a pair of latex gloves and examined the badly swollen area around Lewis's ankle and part of his foot. 'This is very red and angry-looking,' she told him. There were blisters all around the area, as well as bruising beneath the skin, but in the centre there was an area of dead tissue. 'Have you any idea how this happened? Did you graze your ankle at any time?'

Lewis nodded, sinking back against the pillows of the couch. A thin film of sweat beaded his brow, yet his body was racked with cold tremors. 'I caught it on a rock some days ago. It was nothing really, but after the storm it really started to get bad.'

Alyssa reached for her stethoscope and listened to his chest. His lungs were rasping, and when she took his blood pressure she discovered that it was dangerously low.

'Okay, Lewis, I want you to lie back for a while and rest, and I'm going to give you some oxygen to help with your breathing.' She placed an oxygen mask over his nose and mouth and connected it to an oxygen cylinder. 'Take it easy for a while,' she said. 'I'm going to have a word with Dr Blakeley, if that's all right with you.'

He nodded and closed his eyes, and she turned quickly to Ross. 'Would you get him something to drink while I talk to Connor for a moment?' she asked.

'Of course. He's really ill, isn't he?' he said, under his breath.

'I think so, yes. It's good that you brought him to me.'

She glanced at Connor, whose expression was sober as he checked the results on the blood-pressure monitor. 'His pulse is very high,' she murmured, moving away from the couch so that Lewis couldn't hear what was being said. 'And combined with the low blood pressure, I believe he's going into shock. I think we should get him to hospital right away.'

Connor nodded. 'He's dehydrated. Can we get an intravenous line in? And I think it would be wise to give him a strong broad-spectrum anti-biotic. We're looking at sepsis here, and we need to act quickly.'

'Yes, I think you're right about that.' It looked as though Lewis's whole body was inflamed by some sort of infection. 'I'll see to it.'

She'd recognised straight away that it was a grave situation, and for a moment or two she felt the familiar rapid increase in her heartbeat and the knot in the pit of her stomach. Somehow, though, having Connor close by made her feel much stronger, and his presence was reassuring, helping her through this. After a while her hands became steadier and she started to think more clearly.

She said thoughtfully, 'But what could have caused the wound to flare up like that? What kind of organism are we dealing with here? Something waterborne? I know he was standing in flood water next to me the other day, and his legs were bare.' She shook her head. 'I've never seen anything quite like it before. There's an area of dead skin that will need surgical debridement.'

'It could be Vibrio,' Connor said. 'Sometimes after tropical storms it blooms quite profusely in flood water. Molluscs feed on poisonous plankton, and the bacteria can be passed on to people, either through being eaten, if the shellfish aren't prepared properly, boiled, and so on, or they thrive in water and can infect wounds, which is what I think might have happened in this case.'

'And it's more dangerous this way?'

He nodded. 'Extremely so. Lewis is already in a bad way, near to collapse. I think we should take him to hospital now—we can go in my car. It'll be quicker than waiting for an ambulance.'

'Okay. I'll get him ready.'

She set up an intravenous line in Lewis's arm to remedy the dehydration and try to restore the balance of his blood pressure and heart rate, and at the same time she explained to him that they needed to get him to hospital. 'They'll do blood tests and make sure you get the right antibiotic to deal with the infection,' she told him. 'In the meantime, I'm going to inject you with the strongest one I have, and that should help to stop it in its tracks.'

Between them, Ross and Connor helped him out to the car, while Alyssa held the fluid bag of normal saline aloft.

She sat with him in the back of the car while Connor started up the engine. 'Thanks for your help, Ross,' she said, giving him a light wave before the car moved away. Ross was subdued, shocked, she guessed, by what was happening. 'Try not to worry. We'll take care of him.'

Once they arrived at the hospital Connor went into action, hooking Lewis up to a cardiac monitor and checking his vital signs once more. Then he took samples of his blood for testing.

'His breathing's pretty bad,' he said, turning to Alyssa, who was looking on. 'I suspect there's a lot of inflammation there, so I'm going to put him on corticosteroids to try to reduce it. And as soon as I get the test results back, I'll give him electrolytes to restore the acid balance of his blood.' He frowned and turned to the nurse who was assisting him. 'We'll put him on a vasopressor drug and see if that will bring up his blood pressure some more. It's still dangerously low.'

'Okay, I'll get things ready for you.'

A porter took the samples over to the lab and Connor called for a surgeon to come and look at Lewis's wound.

'All we can do now is wait for the results to come through,' Connor told Alyssa some time later. 'It shouldn't take too long for some of the simpler ones to come back from the lab, but he won't be able to go to surgery until we have his condition stabilised.' He glanced at her, taking in her worried expression. 'How are you holding up? Are you okay? I know these situations are worrying for you.'

'I'm all right.' She frowned. 'It's very strange, but for the first time in a couple of years I haven't had that awful, prolonged sick feeling in my stomach when I've had to deal with an emergency. It was there, but it was over very quickly. I can't explain it.' She looked at him. He was so calm, so thorough in everything he did, reliable, capable...everything she dreamed of being.

'Perhaps it was because you were with me,' she murmured as the thought dawned on her. 'I can't think of any other reason why I should feel this way. But around you I feel more secure somehow.'

'Then I'll have to arrange it so that I'm with you more often,' he said with a smile. He wrapped his arms around her and gave her a hug, but it was over almost as soon as it had begun and she mourned the loss of that comforting embrace.

He was called away a few minutes later to deal with another patient, but he urged Alyssa to go and wait in his office. 'I'll come and find you as soon as I have anything for you. I know you're concerned about Lewis. Help yourself to coffee, or whatever. Make yourself at home.'

'I will, thanks.'

She went to his office and made coffee, as he'd suggested, and then sat down to glance through some magazines she found on a low table. She was too anxious about what was happening to Lewis, though, to be able to concentrate for long, and restlessness soon overcame her. She stood up and went to stare out of the window at the fig tree that provided shade in a corner of the landscaped gardens. Everything about Connor's place of work, including the area outside, was designed to be luxurious and peaceful, to put people at their ease.

She turned away and looked around the room. In a corner, on top of a mahogany filing cabinet, she found a child's toy, a lightweight, wooden horse and cart. The wheels on the cart turned when she gently spun them. On the seat of the cart there was a jointed, carved figure of a little girl. Engrossed in the beautiful simplicity of the toy, she took a moment to react when Connor came into the room.

'Oh, you've discovered my secret hobby,' he said, his mouth curving. 'I wasn't sure whether or not to paint it. Do you think it might look better?'

'You made this?' Her eyes widened. 'No, you should leave it. I think it's perfect as it is. I love this sort of thing—in fact, I was just thinking that I'd like to buy something hand-crafted to send home to my mother.' She looked at him with real admiration. 'So this is your hobby?'

'One of them,' he said, nodding. 'The wood's particularly easy to carve. It comes from the gamalamee I was telling you about. It's a kind of balsa wood, so it's really easy to work with. I thought I'd give this toy to the little girl who was nearly drowned. Apparently she lost her doll in the flood—I thought this might help to make up for it.' He frowned. 'What do you think? I wondered if perhaps it's not girly enough?'

She went over to him and laid her hand on his arm, looking up into his eyes. 'Oh, Connor, she'll absolutely love it. I think that's a wonderful idea.'

It was such a thoughtful gesture that it brought a lump to her throat and she wanted to reach up and kiss him…and for a moment or two she was poised on the edge of doing just that. But even as she warred within herself, his arms went around her and he dropped a kiss lightly on her mouth.

'I'm glad you think so,' he murmured.

Flustered, she stayed where she was for the time being, not stirring but watching him, her lips gently parted, stunned by the intimate gesture and desperate for him to sear her mouth with flame once again.

'If you go on looking at me like that,' he warned softly, 'there'll be nothing for it except to kiss you all over again.'

'Um…' She pulled herself together and gave herself a mental shake. What on earth was she thinking? For a second or two she'd been reckless enough to think of throwing caution to the wind and basking in the shelter of his arms. That would have been sheer madness. He would lead her along the same path as all his other conquests and then disentangle himself when he judged things were liable to get out of hand. And she could see them getting out of hand very quickly.

'Did you…?' She tried to collect her thoughts. 'Did you have some news about Lewis? You seem to have been gone for ages.'

'Sorry about that. Yes…' He slowly released her. 'I had some of the results back and added some more drugs to his list of medication. His blood pressure's up a little, so that's a sign things are moving in the right direction, but his heart rate is still very fast. He's not out of the woods yet by a long way. And we need to get that infection under control.'

'I suppose it's something, at least, that his condition isn't getting any worse.'

'Yes. Anyway, he'll be admitted to one of the wards, and another doctor will go on with his treatment.'

He glanced briefly at the wooden cart and then turned back to her. 'How do you feel about going to the market in town to look for that gift you mentioned? My shift's finished so I could take you there, if you like…unless you have to get back for some reason? I can't see that either of us will do any good by staying here any longer— we'll be leaving Lewis in good hands.'

She nodded. 'The filming was due to finish over an hour ago, so I'm through for the day.' She smiled at him. 'I think I'd like that. Thanks.'

They left the hospital a few minutes later after she'd taken a quick look at Lewis to see how he was doing. He was sleeping and his wife was at his bedside. 'I'll leave you two alone,' Alyssa murmured, laying a comforting hand on the woman's shoulder.

'Thank you—both of you—for taking care of him and bringing him here,' the woman said.

'You're welcome. We're very concerned that he should get better.'

They made their way to the car park and set off for the market. It was a short ride away, a bustling place filled with wooden stalls where all kinds of wares were set out. Nearby was an open square bordered with bars and cafés and dotted around with tables and chairs where people could sit to eat and drink. In the middle of the square a traditional steel band was playing. The whole atmosphere was lively and entertaining, and Alyssa felt her spirits lifting.

'I love this market,' she told Connor as they walked around. 'There are so many lovely handcrafted items for sale—I don't know how on earth I'm going to choose what to buy.'

'It's true, they're very big on straw crafts here—handbags, hats, and souvenirs. It depends what you're looking for... Something for your mother, you said?'

'That's right. It's her birthday next week, on Saturday, so I thought I might get her something personal.' There were jewellery stalls full of wonderful necklaces and bracelets made from beads or seeds polished to a high gloss, and some were made of oyster pearls. They stood for a while, watching a woman thread glass beads on to a wire and fashion it into a pretty spiral bracelet.

'She makes it look so easy,' Alyssa said, 'but some of the necklaces she made are very intricate. My mother bought me something similar for my birthday last year...' She smiled. 'It was

funny, because her birthday was a week earlier than mine and I'd bought her a bracelet that
would have gone with it perfectly. She said it gave
her the inspiration for my present.'

'You like jewellery?'

She laughed. 'I do. Show me a woman who
doesn't.'

'Well, yes…' He smiled. 'But I meant, you like
beaded necklaces?'

'Oh, yes. I sort of collect them. I see something pretty like that, and I can scarcely resist
buying it.'

They wandered around the stalls, checking out
the goods, and in the end Alyssa chose a handbag made from woven palm leaves and decorated
with coloured beads. 'I think my mother will like
that,' she said. 'It's lined with silk, and there's a
purse to match.'

'She must look forward to hearing from you,
I expect,' Connor said. 'After all, you've been
here for some time now, and you're a long way
from home.'

'Maybe. I don't really know about that,' Alyssa

answered, a fleeting expression of sadness moving over her features. 'I've tried calling her a few times, but she's usually out—I think she's been especially busy lately, putting together a collection for her boutique.'

'What about your father? Have you spoken to him?'

'A couple of times. He's been away a lot, checking on different subsidiaries of the company, so I've tended to leave email messages instead of phoning these last couple of weeks. That way they get back to me whenever they can.'

He put his arm around her and drew her close. 'I wonder if they know how much you need them to be there for you,' he said softly.

She stared at him, her green eyes troubled. How did he know? It was something she'd tried to keep to herself, this feeling of disconnection from her family. Was he so perceptive that he saw through the outer shell to her inner being?

'I'm a grown woman,' she said. 'They know I'm independent and they probably respect me for it.'

'Maybe.' His arm was reassuringly steady around her, and his hand lightly cupped her shoulder. 'Let's go and get a cold drink and listen to the band for a while.'

'Okay. Just for a half an hour or so, and then I should get back.'

They walked over to the cobbled square and sat at a wooden bench table under the shade of a parasol. A waiter took their order for drinks and Connor ordered a platter of sandwiches. When it arrived a few minutes later Alyssa's eyes grew large. It looked surprisingly appetising.

'I was expecting straightforward bread with a filling,' she said, 'but these look delicious.' Among the sandwiches to choose from there were chicken and bacon with mayonnaise, cheese and sun-dried tomato with a herb dressing, and surrounding it all was a bed of crispy, fresh salad. 'This is wonderful.'

They ate, and drank, and listened to the music, watching as men carried two support struts and a cane into the centre of the square. Then supple limbo dancers dipped and dived, moving around to the heavy beat of the music and taking it in turns to bend beneath the horizontal cane, which was gradually lowered to within a few inches of the ground. The crowd whooped and cheered in delight.

When the show finished, Alyssa glanced at her watch. 'I ought to go back,' she said on a reluctant note.

'Do you have to?'

'I'm afraid so. I've arranged to see Ross later on, back at the house. He said he wanted to talk to me…about the filming, I think. He's very taken up with how it's all going. And he seems to be obsessed with taking on this water-skiing stunt.' She frowned. 'Has he done this sort of thing before?

Connor nodded. 'He's pretty good at all kinds of water sports.' His mouth made a wry curve. 'I think that's how he managed to hook up with quite a few young women—they were very impressed with his prowess…as well as his six-pack.'

'Oh, dear. Even so, even if he's quite skilled, I

still wish he wouldn't do it. I wish Dan had put his foot down and refused to let him take it on.'

She frowned. 'Apparently the scene in the film calls for a race across the water, and I can't help but worry about it. All sorts of things could go wrong—there are bound to be other people and boats on the water, and he could be turned off course by the swell from other boats—not to mention that he's just recovered from a nasty head injury.'

She looked earnestly at Connor. 'Can't you persuade him not to do it? He might listen to you.'

'I can try, but I doubt if he'll take any notice.' His eyes glittered. 'I suspect he's only doing it because he wants to try to impress you. He thinks the world of you.'

'But that's the last thing I want,' she protested, appalled at the thought. 'I hate to think of him risking life and limb for the cameras.'

'Because you care for him, don't you?' Connor's features were in shadow as the sun dipped behind a backdrop of trees. 'You can't bear the thought of him being hurt.'

'Of course I care for him… I think the world of him. He helped me when I was down and encouraged me to come over here—how can I ignore all that now and watch him put himself at risk? He's your brother, don't you want to steer him away from doing anything reckless?'

'There are a lot of things I want,' Connor said darkly, his eyes glinting with some unfathomable emotion. 'And my brother's well-being is one of them. But there are also times when being my brother's keeper can be a bit like wielding a double-edged sword.'

She wasn't quite sure what he meant by that, but she had the feeling that she was at the root of his brooding manner. Was there an inherent rivalry between the brothers that he'd tried to suppress, or was he merely concerned by Ross's apparent foolhardiness?

Either way, she didn't want to be the cause of any dissension between them. What could she do to keep this from happening?

CHAPTER SEVEN

'WELL, there's a sight for sore eyes.' Connor's voice sounded close by and Alyssa woke with a start. She'd been dozing in the hammock outside in the sunshine, and as she looked around, the hammock swayed gently with her movements.

Connor looked as though he was on top form, long, lithe, energetic, dressed in dark trousers and a linen shirt that showed the flat line of his stomach and emphasised his perfect physique.

'I was just… I didn't expect to fall asleep,' she murmured, her voice husky from the heat. It was still before noon, after all, though she glanced at her watch to make sure she hadn't been sleeping for too long. 'I just came out here to take the air for half an hour or so, and before I knew it I must have been well away.'

'Mmm. Perhaps you needed the rest. You

looked so beautifully relaxed, it seemed a pity I had to wake you.' His gaze swept along the length of her, coming to rest on the expanse of her bare thigh, which must have been exposed when she'd wriggled into a more comfortable position. Flustered, she tried to cover herself by quickly tugging down the skirt of her dress.

He pulled a wry face. 'That is such a shame,' he mused on a reflective note, 'I could have stood here and watched you for hours.'

Hot colour ran along her cheekbones. 'You said you had to wake me? Is something wrong?' She sat up, still a bit groggy from sleep, and readied herself to swing down from the hammock. It was the weekend, so there was no work for her to be worrying about, and she wondered what could possibly be the problem.

'Is this to do with Ross? He was going to pick up his new car this morning. He said he would bring it over here to show me...has the deal fallen through somehow?' Ross's car had been a write-off after the accident on the night of the storm, but he'd quickly set about organising a re-placement.

Connor shook his head. 'No, it's nothing like that. Your cousin rang…Carys. You left your phone out on the deck, so I answered it for you in case it was anything urgent. She said she's get-ting an earlier plane and wonders if you could meet her at the airport—she should be arriving in about an hour.' He frowned. 'I'd offer to take you but I have to leave for the hospital around that time. I'm on call with the emergency ser-vices this afternoon.'

'Oh, that's all right, don't worry about it. Thanks, anyway. I have my little runabout and I'm sure I'll manage to find my way to the air-port, even without sat-nav.' She smiled. 'You know Carys, don't you? Ross said you and he were her neighbours when you lived in Florida, though I expect you were all youngsters back then.'

He nodded. 'We've kept in touch with the fam-ily over the years—and we both still go back there quite often.'

'So you'll both probably enjoy seeing her again. Oh, wow… It's great that she's managed to get an earlier flight. I wasn't expecting her to arrive until this evening, but now we'll have a bit more time together. She'll be going back late tomorrow evening.' She pulled in a quick breath. 'I ought to go and give her a ring.'

She went to get down from the hammock, but it started to swing from side to side and she hesitated for a second or two.

'Here, let me help you.' Connor reached for her, his strong arms sliding around her waist and bringing her up close to him. As he lifted her down her soft curves brushed against the length of his hard body, and a whole host of wild and wonderful feelings started up inside her. Blood pumped through her veins with lightning force as she found herself being drawn into his firm embrace, and her whole body was suddenly vibrant with thrilling sensation.

Her feet finally touched the ground, but he went on holding her, and she realised she was in no hurry at all to move away from him. He was tall and strong, impressively masculine, and his powerful arms were locked around her in a way that had every nerve ending clamouring for attention. Delicious tremors shimmered through her. Her breasts were softly crushed against his long, tautly muscled frame, and his strong thighs were pressuring hers, so that a flood of heat began to pool in the pit of her abdomen.

He eased her against him, his hands gently caressing her, gliding along the length of her spine and over the swell of her hips, stirring up a firestorm of heat inside her. Then he bent his head towards her, and she knew that in the very next moment he was going to kiss her. Her heart began to tap out an erratic rhythm, and elation rose up in her. All she could think about was her desperate need to feel his lips on hers.

She didn't have to wait long for her wish to be granted. In the next instant his mouth covered hers, gently coaxing, teasing her lips apart so that in a heartbeat she yielded to the sweet, tender onslaught. Her body was supple, fired up with need, and she moulded herself to him, wanting this moment to never end. Out of the blue, it dawned on her that she'd never felt this way before, never wanted any man the way she wanted him.

'Sweet, sweet girl,' he murmured, nuzzling her throat and trailing a line of flame all the way down to the creamy slope of her shoulder. 'What am I to do? I can't resist you. I'm heady with wanting you, Alyssa. It feels as though I'm drunk and off balance.'

That was how she felt, too, as though her world had been tilted off its axis and she was spinning out of control. It was a strange, breathtaking feeling, and for once in her life she didn't know how to handle things.

She didn't have much time to think about it, though. His head dipped down and in the next moment his lips brushed over the smooth swell of her breasts where they escaped the confines of her lace-edged bra. His kisses were gossamer-light, thrilling her through and through until her whole body tingled with feverish pleasure.

'Heaven knows,' he said in a roughened voice, 'I've tried to keep from doing this, from getting close to you, but it's just too much…it's virtually impossible. You tantalise me…every time I see you, I'm lost…'

His breathing was ragged, his gaze absorbed as his hands moved over her, making a slow, sensual exploration of her rounded curves. Alyssa revelled in his touch. Under the golden blaze of this idyllic island sun everything was perfection and she wanted this moment to last for ever. But she didn't understand what was happening to her. Why did she feel this way? Wasn't it madness to let this go on? Things could very soon get out of hand…

Perhaps she'd been out in the sun too long and the heat had affected her way of thinking. Hadn't he said that all he wanted was a fun, no-strings kind of affair? Was that what she wanted? Would that really be such a bad option? At least she would have him to herself for just a short while.

'I don't know what's happening to me,' she said huskily. 'I've never felt this way before…'

'I know. It's the same for me,' he murmured, his voice rough around the edges. 'I think you've cast a spell on me. I can scarcely think straight when I'm around you.' He gently lifted her hand and placed it over his heart. 'See what you do to me? I don't understand it, no other woman has ever made me feel quite like this before.'

His heart was thudding heavily, a chaotic, thundering rhythm, and she felt its beat ricochet along her arm. Had she really made him feel this way, his emotions raging out of control, just as was happening with her? A short burst of elation spiralled inside her, until she realised her thoughts were taking a hazardous course. Should she stop this right now, or was it already too late? Her heart and mind were at war with one another.

Then the roar of a car's engine sounded in the distance, breaking the spell, and Connor half turned to glance in the direction of the road. 'I guess that must be Ross, coming to show off his new car,' he said on a soft sigh. He ran his hands over her arms. 'Perhaps I should have known I wouldn't get you all to myself for very long.' He lowered his head towards her and kissed her tenderly on the lips. 'Just one more kiss to keep me going…then I'll have that to remember when I'm at work.'

She wound her arms around his neck and kissed him in return. What would it hurt to give way to her feelings just this once?

They drew apart as a car swung onto the driveway of the property. Ross parked by the side of the house and cut the engine.

'What are you two up to?' he said in a suspicious voice, looking them over as he walked towards them. 'You're getting very close all of a sudden, aren't you? Is there something going on that I should know about?'

'You know everything there is to know,' Connor murmured, sliding an arm lightly around Alyssa's waist. He looked at the shiny, metallic grey convertible on the driveway. 'So this is the new dream machine…very nice. From the way you roared in here, I guess you've already put it through its paces.'

Ross smiled, nodding. 'It purrs like a kitten, and the acceleration is so smooth.' He turned to Alyssa. 'I'll have to take you for a spin in it.

You'll love it with the top down and the feel of the wind in your hair. Couldn't be better.' He checked his watch. 'How about now? There's no time like the present.'

'Sorry, but I have to get ready to go and meet Carys at the airport,' she said. 'Perhaps some other time.'

He frowned. 'I could take you there—it's no problem. It's a two plus two seater, so there's room for Carys in the back. She's only a slim slip of a girl, so she should manage okay with a small amount of leg room.' His mouth quirked. 'That's the thing with sports cars…they're built for speed, not space.'

Alyssa thought it over. 'Are you sure you don't mind taking me? It would help as you know the roads better than I do. But I should warn you—I might have to hang around for a while if her plane comes in late. And the journey's more than just a short trip, you know. It will take at least half an hour for us to get there.'

'Or twenty minutes in my new baby.' He gave her a beaming smile.

'Are you planning on writing off this car before you've even had a chance to run it in?' Connor was frowning. 'You'll have Alyssa in the passenger seat—if you're going to drive like a maniac she'll do better to drive herself.'

'Oh, but he wouldn't do that,' Alyssa put in quickly, 'would you, Ross?'

'Of course not, sweetheart.' Ross turned to Connor. 'As if I would do anything to put her at risk. Believe in me, brother. I'll bring her back safe and sound.'

'You'd better. The problem is, I know you too well.' Connor's expression was serious. 'I've been wondering if that knock on your head didn't set off your wild streak, especially after you started to talk about doing the water-ski stunt. You're meant to be the film producer, not the stuntman. The company doesn't insure you to put yourself in the frame.'

Ross reached out and patted him on the shoulder. 'You worry too much, bro. It'll all be fine, you'll see.'

'Hmm.' Connor was still frowning. 'It had

better be. Remember, you have Alyssa to think about—you don't need to be showing off in front of her—she already knows who you are.'

Ross laughed. 'I'll take care of her, I promise.' He looked curiously at his brother. 'Is this a protective instinct coming out in you? I guess I have competition.' He made a crooked smile. 'Still, she already knows you don't have any staying power. I warned her about you and your reputation a long while ago.'

'I'll just bet you did.' Connor's dark eyes glinted, flint-sharp.

Alyssa decided it was time to interrupt. 'Look, you need to put your differences to one side for a while, both of you. And there's no competition going on here. I'm not looking to get involved with anyone. I've been there and it wasn't good, and I'm not likely to be trying it again any time soon, especially with a man who thinks he's the next James Bond and another who thinks the dating game is just that—a game.' Those few minutes in Connor's arms had been a mistake, she could see it now. Why would he think of her differently compared to any of the women who had gone before? She was deluding herself if she thought otherwise, wasn't she?

She was frowning now, and both men were looking at her with alert expressions. She glanced at her watch. 'And I really think I should be setting off or I'll be late. I'll go and get my bag.'

A short time later she slid into the passenger seat of Ross's convertible and watched him set the sat-nav. 'Okay, we're off,' he said, and the engine growled into life. She glanced at him. 'Just kidding,' he murmured. 'Connor's watching, and I wanted to make him sweat.'

'You're such a child,' she scolded. 'Behave yourself, for heaven's sake.' She turned to look at Connor, who was standing by the house, his features taut, his body rigid. She waved, and mouthed silently, 'See you later.'

Ross shot the car along the road, gathering speed until they had left the isolated property behind them. Only then did he slow down and turn to look at her in triumph. 'That gave him something to think about, didn't it?'

'That doesn't even deserve an answer,' she said, flicking him a cool glance. 'You need to grow up, Ross.'

'Yeah, I know. I will.' He slid the car onto the main highway. 'I wouldn't take any risks with you. He ought to know that.' He shot her a quick look. 'But I think you must have crept under his skin somehow and found a soft spot. He's definitely hot and bothered where you're concerned.'

'I doubt it,' she murmured. 'Anyway, could we talk about something else?'

'Sore point, eh?' He smiled. 'Sure. So what do you think of my new beauty? She even has cameras to help with parking. You just switch on the screen on the dash, press "camera", and away you go.'

Alyssa was suitably impressed, and Ross pointed out all the finer features of the car while they drove along. Traffic was building up on the roads, as might have been expected this close to midday, but Ross stayed calm and headed towards the road junction ahead. He glanced in his rear-view mirror.

'Some people are unbelievable,' he murmured, and Alyssa pulled down her courtesy mirror to see what was going on behind them.

A driver in a white saloon was weaving in and out of traffic, as though he was determined to get to the junction ahead of anyone else. He was a young man, in his early twenties, Alyssa guessed.

'He'll end up causing all kinds of mayhem, the way he's going,' Ross murmured. 'I don't see why he can't just…' He let out a mild curse as, without warning, the driver pulled out into the far lane to overtake and then swung back in front of him.

Ross touched his brakes, conscious all the time of the cars closing the gap behind him. 'Now, why on earth would he do something like that?' he murmured, frowning.

'He's obviously in a hurry.'

Too much so, because in the next minute the driver shot across the junction and there was an almighty crash and the awful sound of grinding metal as he ran straight into a car that was already travelling towards the middle of the road.

Alyssa's heart seemed to turn over. 'Oh, no…

Stop the car, Ross,' she said in a shocked voice. 'Is there anywhere you can pull over? I need to go and see if anyone needs help.' It didn't look good. The left side of the other vehicle, a black coupé, had caved in, and the white saloon had lost its front end.

'I can't pull over. I'm completely boxed in,' Ross answered, searching around for a solution. 'The way people drive out here can be awful at times. I'm sorry you had to see this.' He stopped the car next to the crashed cars, and Alyssa slid out of the passenger seat. All the other traffic had come to a standstill and car horns were blaring.

'I don't suppose you have a first-aid box in the car, do you?' she asked, reaching into her bag for her phone as she pushed open the passenger door.

'I do. Connor tells me I always have to be prepared. I'll get it for you.' He stepped out of the car.

'Thanks.' Fumbling around in her bag, she pulled a face. 'I left my phone back at the house. Will you call for an ambulance?'

'Of course. I'm already on it.' He took the first-aid box from the boot of his car and handed it to her, then pulled out his mobile phone and began to punch in numbers.

Alyssa went over to the black car. At first glance that appeared to be the one where there was likely to be the most damage to the occupants.

The woman driver was bleeding badly from a chest wound and appeared to be in deep shock, though she managed to give her name. 'My name is Raeni,' she said. 'My children—' She broke off, struggling to breathe.

Alyssa glanced in the back of the car. There were two children there, a boy and a girl, aged about ten and eight, both white faced and crying quietly. 'Mama's bleeding,' the boy said in a panicked tone, his face crumpling. 'She's bleeding.' The children were very distressed by the sight of the blood.

'I know, but we're going to look after her.' As far as she could tell, neither of the children was injured, but it was clear they were very badly shaken.

'He came out of nowhere,' Raeni managed to say, gasping between each word. 'I don't know what he—' She was very agitated. 'My children—'

'They're all right,' Alyssa assured the woman. 'Try not to upset yourself. Help's on the way.' She took a dressing pad from the first-aid kit. 'I'm going to put this dressing pad against your chest. Perhaps you could hold it there to help stem the bleeding. I have to go and check on the people in the other car, but I promise I'll be back in a minute or two.'

The woman nodded, and Alyssa hurried over to the white saloon. She found the young man slumped over the wheel, but he was still conscious and able to answer Alyssa when she spoke to him. He said his name was Malik. He was alert but breathless, and complained of abdominal pain. There were some cuts on his forearm, too, but nothing that appeared major.

'Try to stay still, Malik,' Alyssa said softly. 'The ambulance will be here soon.' She wished she could give him oxygen, but without her medical equipment she was severely hampered. Added to that, she couldn't split herself two ways and had to decide which person needed attention most of all. She opted to go to the woman in the black car. She was losing blood fairly rapidly and her condition could deteriorate at any moment.

Ross came over to her. 'Can I do anything to help?'

'Yes, please,' she said in a low voice. 'Will you stay with Malik while I see to the other driver? Perhaps you could put a couple of dressings on his arm.' She gave him some dressings and a bandage from the first-aid kit. 'Try to keep him calm, if you can. If he gets agitated it will make his breathing worse.'

'I can do that. Don't worry. I'll stay with him.'

Alyssa went back to the black car but was alarmed to find that Raeni was by now unconscious and the dressing pad was soaked through with her blood. She quickly felt for the pulse at her wrist, but to her dismay it was barely discernible.

She was stunned by what had happened, and

it was the worst kind of situation she could have had to face. If Raeni's heart stopped, or was at a virtual standstill, no oxygen would flow around her body, and she would be brain dead within a very short time unless something was done to save her. What could she do? Where was the ambulance? The thought that she was the only one who could help this woman weighed heavily on her. Was she up to it?

Turning to the children, she said softly, 'I need you to go and sit with my friend for a little while so that I can look after your mother. Will you do that for me? I promise I'll take care of her.'

She bit her lip as she made that promise. Would she be able to save their mother? She shook off the negative thought. She *had* to save her. She couldn't bear the thought of these two innocent children being left motherless.

They tried to object but under her gentle insistence they gradually gave way and she quickly helped them out of the car. Ross gave her a concerned glance. He seemed to understand that she didn't want them to see what she had to do and said, 'Don't worry, they'll be fine with me.'

Alyssa went back to Raeni. Acting on instinct, she lowered the back of the driver's seat so that she was lying as flat as possible. Then she opened the woman's blouse and checked the wound. What she saw almost made her gasp out loud. It was nasty, deep, wide and gaping. How on earth could she bring her through this? She was so badly injured, there was hardly any chance of her being able to pull through.

She was guessing that the wound must have penetrated the heart, but even with the dire prognosis that presented, she couldn't give up, could she? Recalling the children's pinched, tear-stained faces was enough to spur her on. There had to be some way she could restore the woman's circulation.

She switched on the car's interior light so that she would be able to see a little better. She removed a pair of disposable gloves from the first-aid kit, along with a small bottle of antiseptic lotion, then took a sharp pair of scissors from her bag. After dousing the scissors in the solution, she began to clean Raeni's skin. She could only pray that the scissors would be strong enough and sharp enough to do the job in place of a scalpel.

In the distance, she heard the sound of the ambulance as she cut into the woman's chest. There was no anaesthetic she could give her, but in Raeni's present state that was probably the least of her problems. Within a minute or two Alyssa had opened up the area and could see the cause of the problem. The pericardium, the sac around the heart, was swollen and stiff with blood, putting pressure like a clamp around the heart and preventing it from pumping.

She heard the ambulance draw up and soon the paramedics were talking to Ross. She looked around and knew a huge surge of relief as she saw Connor coming towards her.

'Oh, Connor, thank heaven it's you,' she said. 'I'd forgotten it would be you coming out with the ambulance… I'm so glad to see you. I really need your help.' A wave of nausea washed through her as the strain of the last few minutes started to make itself felt on her.

'It's okay, Alyssa… Take it easy… Slow down and take a deep breath…' He laid a reassuring hand on her shoulder. His voice and his calm, soothing presence were instantly comforting to her, and she felt some of the tension ease from her. It was only then, as she looked up at him, that she realised Connor might not be as composed as he seemed. His face was devoid of colour and his body was taut, as though he was steeling himself in some way.

'Are you all right?' she asked, and he nodded.

'Tell me what the situation is here.' His manner was brisk, and that was surely understandable. They were dealing with an emergency here.

'I need to remove the blood clot that's formed in the pericardium,' she told him, 'but she'll need anaesthetic and a fluid line, preferably before I do that. We have to act quickly. She may need medication to force the heart muscle to contract.' She'd find out later what was wrong with Connor. For now, their patient had to be their main priority.

Connor was already opening up his medical kit and pulling on disposable gloves. Within a very short time he had put in an intravenous line so that Raeni could be given life-saving fluids, as well as an anaesthetic and other medication. He put an endotracheal tube down her windpipe and connected it to an oxygen supply.

While he did all that, Alyssa carefully began to remove the blood clot and drained away some of the fluid from the pericardial sac. Slowly, as the pressure was eased, the woman's heart began to beat once more, and at the same time blood began to spurt from the wound site. Alyssa placed her finger over the hole to stem the flow.

'We should get her to hospital right away,' she said. 'I'll keep my finger over the hole until we can get her to a surgeon. Will you phone ahead and arrange for a surgical team to be waiting for us?'

'Yes, I will. Are you going to be okay staying

with her like that? I could take over for you if you like.'

Alyssa shook her head. 'I'll be fine. I'm just anxious about our other patient. He was very breathless. I didn't get a chance to do anything other than check him out.'

'I think the paramedics started to give him oxygen when we arrived, but I'll go and take over from them while we get this lady transferred to the ambulance. Sit tight and I'll send the paramedics over to you.'

'Thanks, Connor.' On an afterthought she said, 'Will you ask Ross to take care of the children and see that they're handed over to their father?'

'I will.' He smiled at her. 'You're doing a great job. You amaze me, Alyssa. You're a brilliant doctor. I'd be more than glad to have you at my side if I were in dire straits. I can't think of anyone else I'd sooner have with me.'

Her heart jumped a little. It was great that he had faith in her. 'Let's hope that's never put to the test.' She stayed where she was, keeping her finger in place to stop the blood from escaping, but his words warmed her through and through.

A couple of minutes later, the paramedics had placed Raeni on a stretcher, and wheeled her to the ambulance, with Alyssa staying constantly by her side, her hand still in position.

Malik travelled with them, propped up a little by pillows to ease his breathing. There was an oxygen mask over his nose and mouth and his eyes were closed, but it was plain to see that he was suffering a considerable amount of discomfort.

'Did you manage to examine him?' Alyssa asked quietly as the ambulance driver started up the engine and they sped away.

Connor nodded. 'I think there may have been some disruption to the diaphragm,' he said in a low voice. 'When I listened to his chest with the stethoscope I could hear sounds that you wouldn't usually expect to hear.'

'You mean there might be a tear in the diaphragm?'

'That's right. So some of the abdominal organs

might have been pushed upwards into the chest cavity. We'll do a chest X-ray and MRI scan to be certain, but I'm pretty sure he'll need surgery.'

Alyssa winced. 'They're both in a bad way.'

'Yes.'

She studied him thoughtfully for a moment or two. 'I didn't realise it straight away, but you weren't quite yourself when you came out of the ambulance. What was wrong?'

'I was fine.'

'No, you weren't. I could tell. What was it, Connor? It couldn't be that you were bothered by the crash, could it? You must have seen things like that many times in your career.'

He nodded, and perhaps he realised that she would persist in her questioning because he said, 'But never when Ross's car was at the scene. When I first stepped out of the ambulance, it looked as though his car was part of the accident. I felt sick to my stomach, imagining that you and he might be injured.'

She sucked in a quick breath. 'I didn't know... I'm so sorry. That must have been awful.'

'It was, but then I found out that you were both okay. That was a tremendous relief. I couldn't bear the thought of either of you being hurt. I don't know how I would have gone on if—' He broke off. He looked uncomfortable, as though he'd said too much.

'If what?' Alyssa prompted him, but he shook his head.

'Nothing. It doesn't matter.'

She thought about it. Was he wondering about how he would go on if anything happened to Ross? Or maybe he was thinking of her…was it possible? Might he care for her more than she dared hope?

Their conversation had to come to an end, though, because by now they had arrived at the hospital and medical teams were waiting in the ambulance bay.

There were separate teams for each of the patients. Raeni was whisked away to the operating theatre and Malik was taken to the radiology department. Alyssa walked with Connor to the emergency room and saw that Raeni's children were there with their father. Ross, it turned out, had gone on to the airport to see if Carys was waiting.

'Heavens, I'd forgotten all about Carys,' Alyssa said in a stunned tone. 'She must be wondering what on earth's going on.'

'I expect Ross will look after her,' Connor murmured.

'Yes, you're probably right.' She was relieved at the thought. 'Perhaps he'll take her for lunch somewhere. That's what I planned to do.'

Connor nodded. 'Don't worry about it—I'm sure Ross will explain the situation to her and help to make her feel welcome. They always got on well together.'

'Good. That's a relief, anyway.'

He led her towards his office. 'I'm still on call for a few hours so I might have to leave at any moment, but I think you should sit down and rest for a while. That must have been a terrible ordeal for you, and yet you stayed in control, doing what you had to do. I'm really proud of you, Alyssa.'

She pressed her lips together. 'I didn't really

get a chance to think about it—until you arrived, and then it hit home with a bang.' They went into the room and he switched on the coffee machine.

'You're a wonderful, skilled doctor,' he said, a few minutes later as he handed her a reviving cup of hot coffee. 'It would be a tremendous waste to the profession if you were to give up on it.'

'I did what I could…but we don't know yet what will happen to her. I may have been too late…'

'At least you gave her a chance of survival. If you hadn't acted as you did, she wouldn't be here now, in the operating theatre.'

Alyssa sipped her coffee. It was good to know that he had faith in her, but could she live up to those expectations? Perhaps it was too early yet to say. She was still very shaken by what had happened.

His pager bleeped and he checked the text message briefly. 'I have to go,' he said. 'Will you get a taxi back home when you're ready? I can give you the number of a reliable company.'

'Yes, I'll be fine. Don't worry about me,' she murmured.

He studied her, his gaze dark and brooding. 'But I do worry,' he said. 'That's the problem.'

CHAPTER EIGHT

'IT MUST have been a terrible shock for you—coming across an accident like that.' Carys shook her head, making her blonde hair swirl silkily around her pretty, oval-shaped face. 'Such awful injuries. Ross has been telling me all about it. And those children—they must have been scared half to death.'

'Yes,' Alyssa agreed, 'that was worrying, seeing how upset they were. It's hard not being able to give them any real news about their mother, but she was still in the recovery room when I left the hospital, and we won't know how she'll be for some time yet. She lost a lot of blood and there are problems with her lungs because of the extent of the injury.'

'At least she came through the operation.' Ross poured drinks for the girls as they sat on the deck, looking out over the sparkling blue ocean. Brown shearwaters swooped and dived for fish, their white underbellies glinting in the sunlight, while black-headed terns cheekily tried to steal their catch.

Alyssa sipped her fruit punch, listening to the clink of ice in her glass. It was good to have Carys here at last. 'Anyway, I'm sorry we had to leave you high and dry at the airport,' she said. 'You must have wondered what was going on. Perhaps you thought we'd abandoned you?'

Carys laughed. 'Oh, no. I knew something must have gone wrong. Ross phoned to tell me he was on his way, and then he took me to the Oasis Club for lunch and drinks. We had a lot of catching up to do, and he told me all about the filming.' She frowned. 'Apparently it will all be over with soon... I expect life will seem fairly drab after all the excitement of the film shoots.'

'You're probably right. I think Ross will feel it quite badly—he thrives on the adrenaline rush.'

Ross nodded agreement. 'Once one project finishes, I'm on the lookout for another.'

As for herself, she would have to think through her options once her contract with the company came to an end. Instead of the relatively easy time she had been expecting, this stint of work in the Bahamas had given her a lot of food for thought.

They chatted through the afternoon, until Connor arrived home from his shift with the ambulance service.

'Hi, there, Carys,' he said, coming on to the deck and greeting her with a warm smile. 'It's good to see you again.' He bent his head towards her.

'You, too.' Carys lifted her cheek for his kiss and, watching them in such a warm, tender embrace, Alyssa felt a sudden sharp stab of jealousy. It was an unexpected reaction and definitely one that she didn't want. It was upsetting that she should respond this way, and it bewildered her. After all, there was no call for it—Carys was her cousin, they'd been close friends all their lives, like sisters almost, and it was perfectly natural for her and Connor to be close to one another.

Even so, she bent her head to hide her frown. Had her cousin kissed Ross that way, or were these special moments reserved for Connor?

Annoyed with herself, she swallowed some more of her ice-cold drink and put on a smile. 'We were wondering what to do this evening,' she told Connor. 'We thought it might be good to take Carys somewhere special.'

He straightened up and nodded. 'I've been thinking about that. There's a beach barbecue and fire-eating show going on tonight at Smugglers' Cove. That should be well worth a visit.'

'It sounds great,' Carys said, her blue eyes bright with anticipation. 'I vote we go for the fire-eating—just as long as I don't have to try it out myself!'

'I doubt there's much chance of that.' Connor laughed. 'But it should be fun, and there's usually dancing and a whole variety of cocktails to try out.'

'You're leading me down the path to devil-may-care, I can see that,' she told him with a smile.

'But I'm not worried. I'm here to relax and have a good time, and I want Alyssa to do the same.'

'Oh, I will,' Alyssa murmured. 'I'm there in spirit already.' She shot Connor a quick look. 'Why is it called Smugglers' Cove—were there dark and dangerous goings on there at some time in the past?'

'There certainly were. It was the hub of rum-running in the prohibition era. There are lots of caves around there where sailors could hide their booty.'

She smiled. 'It's getting to sound more and more interesting.'

'You'll enjoy it, I'm sure.' Connor went to shower and change, and later, as the sun started to set on the horizon, they all set off to walk along the headland to Smugglers' Cove. Rounding the bay, they were met by the sound of drums beating out a fast, heady rhythm and by the sight of islanders dressed in vivid costumes, dancing to the feverish beat.

The aroma of barbecued chicken greeted them, and a buffet table had been laid out on a terrace filled with platters of pork, ribs, rice and peas and bowls of salad. It was colourful and appetising, and Alyssa realised she was hungry.

Connor and Ross went to get drinks while the girls found seats at a table and sat down to watch the dancers. Men, bare-chested and athletic, moved to the music, their bodies supple and toned, while the women dancers wore tube tops and flouncy short skirts that flicked up and down as they shifted to the rhythm of the band. There was a fire at the centre of the group, and they took it in turn to light torches, swirling them around, making patterns with the flames.

Alyssa drank tequila sunrise, a flamboyant cocktail with brilliant red and orange colouring, and felt the music deep down inside her, so that when the floor show finished and Connor held out his hand to draw her to her feet, she was ready to dance with him in the traditional hip-shaking, foot-stomping way of the fire dancers. They laughed together, buoyed up by the cheerful atmosphere, and when Carys and Ross came to join them they danced as a foursome.

'I'd no idea you could move like that,' Alyssa remarked, and Connor smiled and tugged her to him.

'You don't do so badly yourself,' he murmured huskily against her cheek. 'You've been tantalising me all night long with those swaying hips and that gorgeous body.'

'Have I really?' She laughed, snuggling up to him. Perhaps the alcohol had gone to her head because all she wanted right now was to be in his arms and it didn't matter to her that there were people all around.

'Yes, you have, Jezebel.' His eyes were dark, glittering with smouldering intent. 'I've been wanting to get close to you all night. I need to have you all to myself.' He looked around. 'What do you say we give these two the slip and go for a walk along the beach?'

'That sounds good to me.' She glanced over to where Ross and Carys were engrossed, deep in conversation. 'I don't think they'll miss us, do you?'

'It doesn't look like it. They've really hit it off, haven't they?'

So they set out to walk back along the beach in the moonlight, kicking up the sand with their bare feet, laughing when the waves rolled in and tickled their toes.

'I think I've had too much to drink,' she murmured, gazing up at the clear night sky. Stars shimmered like diamonds and in the balmy evening the whole world seemed magical. 'My head is swirling, and it's filled with music.'

'That's because we can still hear it, even from this distance.' They rounded the headland and stood for a while, looking out over the bay. A heron was silhouetted against the moonlit horizon, standing on a rocky outcrop, preening itself.

Connor took her in his arms and kissed her tenderly, and it seemed to Alyssa just then that it was so right that they should be together like this. No one had ever made her feel so good, so perfectly at ease with herself and the world.

'Have you had a good time tonight?' he asked

softly, and she nodded, blissful in his arms, not wanting to move.

'I have. I think I've fallen in love with this island, its people and their traditions.' She'd probably fallen in love with him, too, and maybe that was what coloured her judgement, but she couldn't tell him that. He might feel it was time to gently extricate himself, and she wanted to stay close to him for as long as was possible.

'I'm glad. I want you to be happy, Alyssa. You were so sad when you first came here… Not outwardly, but I think inside you were hurting, though I didn't realise it at the time. You talked about how you felt about your work, your relationship with your parents, and your ex… Do you still feel bad about breaking up with him?'

She shook her head. 'I haven't thought about him in a long time.' She frowned. 'It's strange, isn't it, how someone can take up so much of your thoughts and be so great a part of your life, and yet after a while they fade into the distance?' She thought about that for a while.

'I think perhaps we were never really suited.

He didn't understand me and how important my work was to me back then. And, of course, when everything went wrong for me in my job, he wasn't there to support me. I suppose I started to look at him with different eyes then, even before he cheated on me.'

Thinking about that was a salutary reminder of how things could go wrong. She looked up at Connor, his face shadowed in the moonlight. Could she let herself love him and put her trust in him? She wanted to, so much.

He cupped her cheek in his hand. 'I shouldn't have doubted you when you first came here. I had such pre-set ideas about the women who'd set their sights on Ross in the past, and I was judging you without even knowing you.'

'And you don't have those same worries about Carys?' She smiled. 'He seems to be very taken with her.'

'He's always had a place in his heart for Carys. Nothing ever came of it because she sees him for what he is—a man who enjoys life to the hilt and jumps at every opportunity without thinking first.'

'Perhaps he's changing.'

'Maybe.'

'So you don't need to be his protector any more?'

'Probably not. It's a habit I should have left behind long ago.' He smiled. 'I wonder why we're wasting this moonlit night talking about Ross?'

She knew the answer to that. 'Because I've had a little too much to drink and I'm afraid if I let you kiss me I'll do something foolish like fall in love with you.'

He inhaled sharply. 'That would never do, would it?'

'No.' She shook her head. 'You know what they say, "once bitten…"'

'True. But not all relationships have to end badly, do they? Perhaps I hadn't thought about it properly before. I mean, just because your ex let you down, and my parents made a mess of things, it doesn't have to follow that all love affairs follow the same course, does it?'

He swooped to claim her mouth once more and kissed her, deeply, passionately with all the fervour of a man whose emotions were rapidly running out of control. His hands shaped her and drew her to him, tracing the lines of her body with tender devotion.

'I want you so much...' he said raggedly '...so much that it's like an ache deep inside me.'

Her heart seemed to flip over. It was good to know that she could make him feel this way... It made her blood fizz with excitement and filled her with exhilaration to know that he wanted her, and in her heady, dreamlike state she was almost ready to throw caution to the winds and tell him she felt the same way. But self-preservation was a powerful deterrent and just a hint of caution remained, a tiny spark of doubt left to torment her. Perhaps his view of things was changing, but he still talked about affairs, and not about a lasting commitment, didn't he?

It would hurt her so badly if he were to cast her aside once she had committed herself to him. She knew it and there was no escaping the fact. The distress of having to end the relationship with James would be nothing compared to how she would feel if Connor was to go out of her life. She realised now that her feelings for him went very deep, deeper than she'd ever thought possible, and she didn't think she could cope if he were to let her down.

'Alyssa…'

'I know,' she said softly, on a breathy sigh. 'I want you too, but I need to get my feelings straight. I can't let you sweep me off my feet.'

'Are you sure about that?' His lips gently nuzzled the curve of her neck, and slid down along the bare slope of her shoulder. 'It's a very tempting idea. You know there's nothing I'd like more. Ever since the accident, I've been thinking about you and me…how we might be together…'

But before he could kiss her again they heard the sound of voices in the distance, coming ever closer, and Connor sighed and rested his cheek against hers for a second or two. Then he straightened and reluctantly eased himself away from her, still holding onto her hands and looking around to see who was coming along the path towards them.

Alyssa's mind was in a whirl. What did he mean, how they might be together?

'I might have known,' he said, under his breath. 'Ross's timing has always been atrocious.'

'I suppose they decided it was about time to set off for home,' Alyssa murmured, watching his brother and Carys coming closer. 'The music has stopped. It must be very late.'

He laid an arm around her shoulder. 'You're right. I guess we should be thinking about what we can do to entertain Carys tomorrow...unless you want to keep her to yourself?'

She shook her head. 'I think she'd enjoy the four of us being together.' She felt the loss of his arms around her intensely, and she was churned up inside at the interruption, but Carys had come over here especially to see her, and now she felt guilty because of her own dismay at seeing her turn up on the footpath with Ross. She wanted to be alone with Connor right now...but maybe that was not the most sensible idea around.

They went back to the house with Ross and Carys, and since it was so late Ross decided to stay in his brother's apartment overnight.

In the morning, they all had breakfast together on the deck outside Connor's apartment.

'I thought you might like to take a trip around the islands,' Connor suggested, looking first at Carys and then at Alyssa. 'My yacht's moored not far from here—we could spend the day seeing the sights from on board, take a picnic lunch with us. What do you think?'

'That sounds wonderful.' Carys glanced at Alyssa and she nodded in agreement.

'I think so, too. Perhaps we'd better start getting some food together…and maybe a bottle or two or three…'

Connor shook his head. 'There's no need for you to do that. I'll organise things. You two can just relax and spend some time together while Ross and I see to everything.'

'Well, I'm all for that,' Carys murmured, smiling. 'I'll go and put on some sun cream in readiness.'

'Me, too.' Alyssa turned to go downstairs with Carys, picking up her phone as its ringtone sounded.

She was startled to hear her mother's voice on the other end of the line.

'Hi, Mum, how are you doing?' She signalled to Carys that she was going to take the call out in the garden, and Carys gave her a cheery wave in return.

'I just heard all about the accident you were caught up in,' her mother said, sounding vexed. 'Why on earth didn't you tell me about it?'

'The accident?' Alyssa was puzzled. How would her mother come to know anything about what had happened? Which accident was she talking about?

'On the night of the storm. The car was a write-off, but you didn't say a word. Heavens, Lyssa, you could have been hurt…but you didn't tell me. I'm your mother, and I knew nothing at all about it.'

'I'm sorry. I was fine and I thought it best not

to worry you.' She frowned. 'How did you get
to hear about it?'

'Well, you know how it is. Your Aunt Jenny
heard it from Carys…and Jenny is my sister, after
all, so she phoned me and asked, did I know? Of
course I didn't. You never tell me anything.'

'That's not true,' Alyssa protested. 'I email you
lots of times and tell you all the gossip—I just
don't mention anything that might worry you un-
necessarily, that's all.'

'Well, you should have told me about that.' Her
mother was indignant. 'I need to know that you're
safe.'

'I am. Honestly. I'm fine. You've no need to
worry about me. It was poor Ross who came out
of it with concussion, but he's okay now.' Alyssa
was touched that her mother had taken the trouble to phone her. 'I miss you, Mum. It's great to
hear from you.'

'We miss you, too, Lyssa. Maybe your dad
and I could have a video chat with you when it's
your birthday next week? We must arrange a time
that's good for the three of us.'

They talked for a few more minutes and Alyssa promised she would let her mother know straight away if anything out of the ordinary happened. In turn, her mother said she would try to keep in touch more often.

'We'll choose a time each week when we can be sure we're both able to get to the phone,' she said. There was a wistful note in her voice as she added, 'Though it would be good if we were able to see you again properly. I couldn't quite take it in when you suddenly upped and left, but your father and I didn't want to stand in your way.'

It was strange, hearing things from her parents' point of view, and when she cut the call a short time later, Alyssa was deep in thought.

'Is everything all right?' Connor asked, on his way from the house to the car with a large wicker hamper. 'Did I hear you say it was your mother on the phone?'

'Yes, it was…and everything's fine. She heard about Ross's car being written off and wanted to know what happened. She said they miss me.

She and Dad are going to call me on my birthday—they want to do a video call that morning.'

His mouth curved. 'That sounds good. Perhaps it won't seem so bad being far away from them if you can hook up by video and actually get to see one another.'

She nodded. 'I suppose so. Though with my contract coming to an end soon I'll have to decide what I'm going to do…whether to stay on here and look for work or maybe go back home. I think my parents would like that.'

He set the hamper down on the ground. He appeared to be stunned. His body became rigid, his shoulders stiff and his whole frame was tense. 'You're not really thinking of going back home, are you?' he said in a shocked voice. 'I thought you said you loved the island?'

Her eyes were troubled. 'I do. But I have to be practical and think about the future. When I came here I needed a break, time to sort myself out. I was trying to decide whether I should give up on medicine altogether. I'm still not entirely sure, but I don't think I can go on straddling the fence for much longer. And if I choose medicine… Well, the fact is I did my training in the UK, so it would seem sensible to go back there to work.'

She didn't tell him the one true factor that would underline her decision-making. She wanted to be near to Connor, to spend her days—and nights—with him. But his track record wasn't encouraging where women were concerned and she'd already seen for herself that things could go badly wrong. Maybe she would feel differently if he gave her some idea that he wanted more than a fleeting affair, but why would he change the habit of a lifetime?

'I can't imagine how it would be without you here,' he said huskily. 'I've grown so used to having you around. You can't mean it…'

'I have to consider it as a real possibility,' she said. She was surprised by how much her words seemed to have affected him. The colour had drained from his face. 'But I still have a week or so before I need to make my decision.'

He nodded, and she said quietly, 'I suppose I

should go and get ready for this boat trip. I'm already running late, from the looks of things.' She gestured towards the hamper. 'Have you filled that up already? Surely, you haven't had time?'

'No. That's true, we haven't.' He seemed to make a conscious effort to relax his stance. 'I phoned the catering service in the town and they're going to fill the basket for me. It's only a ten-minute run in the car, so I'll be back before you know it.' His gaze wandered over her. 'You look as though you're ready for the day ahead, anyway. You're perfect as you are.'

'Well, thanks for the vote of confidence.' She smiled. She had chosen to wear white jeans and a lightly patterned blouse that was gently nipped in at the waist. 'I'll just put on some more lipstick and pin back my hair, and then I'll be ready to go. We won't keep you waiting.'

'That's all right. Don't worry about it…but your hair looks great as it is. It always looks good, whether you leave it loose or pin it up, or whatever. I've always thought it was beautiful…that glossy, deep chestnut colour and those gorgeous curls. You look fantastic.'

She felt warm colour run along her cheekbones. 'I'm glad you feel that way. Somehow, with Carys around, looking so lovely, I sometimes feel as though I fade into the background. She's truly beautiful.'

He reached for her, his hands lightly clasping her bare arms. 'So are you. You could never fade into the background. Don't even think it.' He frowned, looking her over. 'You don't have much self-confidence, do you? And yet you have so much to be proud of. All that nonsense about leaving… Maybe I can help you to change your mind.'

She shook her head. 'I don't think that will work,' she said.

'No?' A challenging glint came into his eyes. 'I can see I'm going to have to take you in hand.'

She glanced at the fingers curled around her arms. 'Did you mean that literally?'

'Oh, yes. Definitely.' He had started to pull her

towards him when Ross shouted down from the upper veranda.

'Are you going to get that hamper filled,' he said with an amused twist to his mouth, 'or are we going to hang about all morning? Stop fooling around, bro, and get a move on.'

Connor's mouth quirked in mock annoyance. 'I knew I should have sent him back to his own place last night.'

Alyssa chuckled, faintly relieved by the diversion. After all, she couldn't be certain she would be able to withstand Connor's gentle coaxing. 'There are times when I think I must be lucky not to have any siblings. People talk about rivalry, and you expect it when they're young, but when you grow up…?'

'Yeah, well, a lot of testosterone gets thrown about where men are involved.' He let her go and went to load the hamper in the car. 'I won't be long,' he promised.

He was as good as his word, and it was around mid-morning when they set sail from the marina where Connor's yacht was moored. They climbed into the boat and within a very short time they were cruising the crystal clear waters around the island, with Connor at the helm. Ross mixed rum punch and offered the girls the chance to look through his binoculars at the startling white cliffs in the distance.

After a while, Alyssa went to join Connor at the helm. She handed him an ice-cold lager and he swallowed the drink gratefully.

'Thanks, I was ready for that.'

'I thought you might be.' She pointed to the island in the distance. 'Is that where we're headed?'

'Yes, Ross and I thought it would be a good place to stop for lunch. There's a lovely stretch of beach in a sheltered bay—it's fringed by coral reefs, so it's really one of the most beautiful places around.'

'From what I've seen, the coral is spectacular,' she murmured. 'I didn't think we'd be able to get so close to it, but in these calm waters you can see everything.' She'd seen swaying purple sea fans, pink sea anemones and myriad brightly coloured tropical fish.

'I hoped you would like it,' he said, smiling.

'I do.' She sighed contentedly. 'I'm so glad we came out here today. I wanted to see as much as I could of the reefs and the fish that swim around them. Carys said she was keen on doing that as well.'

'You should have a good chance of that this afternoon.'

They moved slowly through the sparkling turquoise water for an hour or so, and then dropped anchor in the bay of the island they had seen some time ago through the binoculars.

From the deck of the yacht Alyssa looked out at the pristine white sand that bordered the cliffs. Long-billed pelicans made their nesting ground near rocky outcrops, and overhead they could hear gulls calling to one another.

Connor opened up the hamper and produced a wonderful selection of food. There were spiced meats and rock lobster, along with pâté and savoury biscuits, salad and a variety of mouth-watering dips. For dessert they ate fruit tarts with fresh cream—everything had been kept chilled in a cooler and had then been transferred to the fridge on board the yacht.

'Mmm…I could get used to this life,' Alyssa murmured, leaning back in her seat and sipping the highball Ross had handed her.

'Me, too.' Carys stretched out her long, slender legs. 'I've eaten way too much.' She gave Connor a mock glare. 'You're using this weekend to ply me with food—I shall soon be totally fat.'

He laughed. He was sitting by the deck rail and now he cast a glance over her lithe body. 'Oh, I don't think so,' he said. 'You've had that same figure for the last several years—I doubt you're going to start piling on the pounds now.'

'Huh. So you say. How am I supposed to do any work tomorrow? I shall still be stuffed by morning, and it's all your fault for providing such luscious food.'

'Ah, well, I dare say the events management team can do without your input for a few hours… if the local sports club doesn't get their programme for the charity fete for another day or so, it's hardly going to matter, is it? And if Ross's film schedule's held up for half a day because he can't get out of his chair, no one will worry too much.'

'Don't you believe it,' Ross interjected drily. 'The finance department will be on my tail for a week or more.' He made a wry smile. 'Still, I don't suppose it's quite the same as you and Alyssa not turning up for work, is it?'

'I'm not so sure about that,' Alyssa murmured. 'We're not indispensable. There will always be someone skilled and capable who can look after the patients for us.' She looked at Connor. 'Not that I'm suggesting we leave them to it,' she added.

'I don't know,' Ross said. 'If you hadn't been there when those two cars crashed, I doubt Raeni would still be with us. How is she? Do you know?'

'She's still sedated and recovering from the loss of blood,' Connor said, 'and from the fact that her heart actually stopped beating at one point. They haven't managed to restore her heart to a normal rhythm yet, so that's a worry, but she's in

Intensive Care, so everything's being done that can be done.'

Alyssa swirled the colourful juice in her glass. 'Did you get to hear anything more about Malik? I rang up yesterday to try and find out, but the consultant was still deciding on the best course of action.'

'There was a tear in his diaphragm,' Connor told her. 'They've decided to operate tomorrow, so we should know a bit more by late afternoon.'

Carys frowned. 'I could never do that job,' she said quietly. 'It would worry me way too much.'

Alyssa nodded. 'That's how I felt when I came over here. I didn't know if I would be able to go on working as a doctor—I thought these last few months would give me the break I needed to help me recharge my batteries.' She frowned. 'But then we had to deal with some real emergencies—something I never expected to happen—and I began to think my career was over. I didn't think I could cope.'

'Do you still feel that way?' Connor was standing by the deck rail, watching her closely.

She shook her head. 'I think I've discovered that I would far rather try to save lives than not to try at all.' She was thoughtful for a moment. 'Things don't always work out the way we want them to in this job, but at least we have the satisfaction of doing everything we possibly can.'

He came over to her and reached for her hand. 'I'm really glad you feel that way,' he said, going down on his haunches beside her. 'I think you've made the right decision.'

She made a faint smile. 'I wasn't so keen when Alex fell from the lorry,' she said quietly. 'But he's beginning to make good progress with his walking, so I guess things are looking up for him at last.'

Lewis hadn't been quite so lucky, though. She'd looked in on him a couple of days ago and the consultant in charge of his case was still searching for a strong antibiotic that would knock the septicaemia on its head. The ones they'd tried so far weren't bringing about the response the team had hoped for.

'Alex should come out of this without any lasting effects,' Connor said. 'He looked really cheer-ful when I last saw him.' He stood up, glancing out over the side of the yacht and began to tug on her hand, urging her up from her seat. 'Come and see this... I think a shoal of fish must be head-ing our way. You, too, Carys. You might want to see this.'

They all went with him to the deck rail, Ross coming to stand beside Alyssa, while Connor pointed out the shoal to Carys.

'They don't usually come this close to the sur-face,' he said softly.

'What are they?' Carys asked. 'Do you know?'

'They're parrotfish—they call them that be-cause of their parrot-like beaks.'

'Oh, I've heard about them,' Carys said, in-trigued. 'They use the beak to scrape off coral so that they can feed on algae. They're beautifully coloured, aren't they?' They were blue, yellow and red, flashing brightly as they swam through the water in search of coral. 'I heard they can change sex,' she added in an awed voice. 'That must cause some confusion among the ranks.'

They all laughed and went to sit back on deck. They sipped cocktails and chatted for some time, until Carys reluctantly mentioned that she had a plane to catch in a couple of hours.

'Okay, we'll up anchor,' Connor said. 'I'll drive you to the airport, if you like.'

'Okay, thanks.'

Ross frowned, and Alyssa wondered if he was troubled by his brother's offer. He didn't say anything, though, and when they arrived back at the house some time later, Ross went into the study in Connor's apartment and left Connor to make the arrangements for the journey to the airport. 'I have to make a phone call,' he told Carys. 'You won't leave without saying goodbye, will you?'

'Of course not.' Carys went with Alyssa to the ground-floor apartment. 'I'll be ready in a jiffy,' she told Connor. 'My bag was almost packed before we went out this morning, so I've only a few things to add to it.'

'That's okay. I'll be out on the deck when you need me.'

Alyssa's phone bleeped and she checked the

text message that had arrived as they'd walked into the sitting room. 'My mother's arranged a time for us to link up by phone once a week,' she said, looking pleased. 'I wondered if she would remember.'

She chatted with Carys as her cousin finished putting last-minute items into her bag.

'Connor's gorgeous, isn't he?' Carys said, looking around for her make-up bag. 'I was thrilled to bits that he took us out on the boat today. I really wasn't expecting anything like that—just you and me together and a few take-away meals was what I thought when we planned the weekend—and then he went and produced that luxury hamper. Wow, that's the life, isn't it? It'll seem so mundane, going back to my little home in Florida.'

'Yes, I know what you mean.' Alyssa could well understand her cousin's enthusiasm. 'But you do love your home really, and your family is there…that must count for a lot.'

'True.' Carys sighed. 'But he is great, all the same.'

Alyssa chuckled. 'Don't tell me you're smitten.

It seems to happen to an awful lot of women, from what I've heard.'

'Yeah…fat chance I'd have there.'

'Anyway, Ross is just as dishy, and he's very keen on you, or hadn't you noticed?'

'Ross?' Carys's eyebrows shot up. 'No way. You're joking.'

'I'm not.'

'You are, too.'

Still exchanging banter, the girls set off to meet Connor up on the deck.

'Oh…I think I left my phone somewhere,' Alyssa said. 'I'd better go and find it.' She was thinking of going with Carys to the airport, so she would need to have her bag as well. 'I'll catch up with you,' she said.

'Okay, no worries.'

It took a few minutes for Alyssa to find her phone, but eventually it turned up beneath a couple of magazines that Carys had put to one side while she was collecting her things together.

She dropped it into her bag and went upstairs to join Connor and her cousin.

She'd expected to hear them talking, but as she approached the veranda from Connor's sitting room she saw that they were very quiet, talking in hushed tones and standing by the rail, their heads close together. Connor put his arm around Carys's shoulder, bending his head towards her, and it seemed at one point as though their bodies almost meshed together.

Alyssa watched them, her mind reeling in stunned surprise. Connor's expression was serious, and Carys was looking up at him with rapt attention.

Alyssa felt a wave of nausea wash over her. Was this really happening? She hadn't mistaken what she'd seen, had she? Now all her dreams were dissolving in the light of that close embrace.

Was he exactly as people had implied, a man who went from one woman to the next? How could he do this? How could he tell her how much he wanted her, make her yearn for him in return, and then casually move on to try his charm on another woman?

He was treating her feelings as if they were of no account, trampling all over them.

She couldn't bear to watch. This hurt went deep, like a knife wound to the heart, and her whole body froze in pain. Her world had collapsed in an instant. What was she to do now?

CHAPTER NINE

'I'LL miss you, Alyssa.' Carys stood beside Connor's car and gave Alyssa a hug. 'We'll have to meet up again soon.'

'We will.' Alyssa was still hurting inside from the shock of seeing her cousin in such an intimate embrace with Connor, but none of this was her cousin's fault so she made an effort to put on a show of cheerfulness. 'I'll come over to Florida for a weekend before I go…and there's always the gala dinner in a few days' time, on Saturday. You have to come over for that.'

Carys nodded with enthusiasm. 'Yes, I'll be there.'

Ross came to say his goodbyes, and Alyssa noticed he held onto Carys's hand for a fraction longer than necessary. 'I was going to offer to take you to the airport myself,' he said, 'but Connor beat me to it. I think I hate him.'

Carys laughed. 'Don't feel so bad about it. There'll be other times. Anyway, I think he wants to talk to me about something—events management stuff for the hospital, and so on, and we can do that on the way.'

'Oh, boring stuff...' Ross grinned and kissed her lightly on the cheek. 'Bye, Carys.'

'Bye, Ross. And if you even think of doing that stunt with the water-skis, I shan't speak to you. It was bad enough hearing that you'd been virtually knocked unconscious. You've been warned.'

Ross's brows lifted. 'So you do care about me after all? Okay, I won't do it, then. I promise.'

Smiling, Carys slid into the passenger seat beside Connor. Alyssa didn't think for a minute that Connor planned to talk to her about events management, but there was definitely some reason why he'd been so quick to offer to drive her to the airport. She had no idea what that might be, but she was determined now that she wasn't going to go with them to find out. There was the problem of two's company, three's a crowd, to make her think twice about doing that.

But she was still deeply troubled by what she'd seen earlier. Connor had obviously been concerned when she'd said she was thinking about going back to the UK, and perhaps he'd taken that to mean he would have no chance with her. It seemed a bit odd that he should turn his attention to Carys so soon, though, especially since it was clear that Ross was interested in her.

She waved Carys off and went to her bedroom. There, she lay on the bed and tried to think things through. Connor had never looked at another woman in all the time she'd been over here. It just didn't add up that he should start doing it now.

Could it be that she'd misinterpreted his actions? Perhaps she was letting her ex's behaviour influence her unduly. She had a huge problem with trust, and it had coloured all her judgement. But she couldn't rid herself of that image of Connor with his arm around Carys. It had shocked her to the core.

The situation tormented her, and she had no

idea how to resolve the problem. She loved Connor, she realised that now, but it was like a festering wound, believing that he had let her down so badly.

Over the next few days, she couldn't eat, she couldn't sleep, but she tried to lose herself in work, anything to blot out the picture of Connor and Carys together. She couldn't bring herself to talk to him about her worries because he might tell her it was true, and she didn't know how on earth she would handle that without falling apart. It would be a crippling blow.

She went through the motions at work, putting on a brave face for the occasional patient who came into her surgery. When she had some free time she went over to the hospital to look in on the people she had treated.

'Raeni's on the mend, I believe,' the registrar told her. 'Her breathing's improved, and her heart is pumping much more strongly. She seems to have turned the corner.'

'That's brilliant news,' she said, relieved. Apparently Raeni's children went to see her every day with their father, and were beginning to talk about the day when she would go home.

'It shouldn't be too much longer now,' the registrar added, 'two or three weeks, maybe. Of course, she'll have to take things easy to begin with, while everything continues to heal.'

'That's much better than I expected, anyway.' Alyssa thanked him and went to check on Malik, who was recovering on the men's ward after his surgery.

'How are you doing?' she asked him. 'I hear the operation went well.'

'I'm okay…a bit sore, but the doctor said that's to be expected. I got them to take me over to see the lady who was in the other car. I'm really sorry for the way she was hurt.' He pulled a face. 'I was in a hurry that day because my wife rang to say she'd gone into labour. I was trying to get back home to her.'

'I'm sorry things turned out the way they did.' Alyssa frowned. 'What happened when you didn't get home?'

'A neighbour took her to the hospital.' He grinned, showing white teeth. 'We have a little girl. She's beautiful.'

'I'm glad it worked out all right, in the end, Malik. Congratulations.'

Back on the film set, things were winding to a close. They finished filming the water-ski chase, and she was glad to see that Ross stood back and let a professional stuntman do the action scenes.

'I didn't have much choice,' he told her in a mournful voice. 'I'm pretty sure Carys meant what she said when she told me she wouldn't speak to me. I guess my wild days are over.'

'Poor you.' She patted his shoulder and sent him a commiserating glance. 'You'll have to settle for being a top-notch film producer instead.'

'Yeah.' He laughed. 'I guess that's not so bad.'

A couple of days after that Alyssa closed down her medical centre and locked the door on what had been her sanctuary for the last few months. In a way, she was sad to see it come to an end, but she'd learned a lot about herself and her vocation as a doctor since she'd been here. It had given her a good breathing space and allowed her to sort out what she needed to do next.

On the day of the gala dinner she awoke to a glorious, sun-filled day and decided to go for a walk along the beach before breakfast. It would give her time to think. She needed to sort things out, once and for all.

She gazed around her at the gently swaying branches of the palm trees and let her glance wander over the magnificent sweep of the bay, where the blue water of the ocean met smooth, white sand. It was flawless, a true paradise island...all it needed was for her to find her soul-mate and to live with him here in perfect harmony.

She smiled wistfully and watched the waves break on the shore, leaving lacy ribbons of white foam. She desperately wanted Connor to be there with her.

Over these last few days she'd had plenty of time to think about what had happened on the day when he had taken Carys to the airport. Wasn't it possible she'd got the wrong end of the stick and come up with a false idea of what was going on? Back home, her ex had cheated on her, and ever since then she'd found it hard to put her trust in anyone.

But James was a totally different person from Connor, wasn't he? He'd never been particularly supportive, or understanding, whereas Connor had been there for her every step of the way. He'd never let her down. In fact, he'd gone out of his way to make sure she was safe, happy, and even that she was secure in her work.

She loved him, and surely that meant she had to learn to trust him? Somehow or other, she had to take risks with her feelings, because she didn't want to miss out on being with him.

'Alyssa…'

It was as though, by thinking of him, she'd somehow managed to conjure him up. She shielded her eyes against the sun and looked to-wards the house, to see Connor coming down the path that led to the beach.

'Hi.' She waved, and waited for him to come closer. 'You're up and about early,' she said. 'I thought this was your day off? I expected you'd be having a lie-in.'

'It is.' He caught up with her and came to stand alongside her, looking out over the sea. 'I heard you moving chairs about on the deck and I realised you'd been going off for early morning walks since your work here finished. I wanted to come with you and wish you a happy birthday.'

Her eyes widened. 'I didn't think you would remember.'

He smiled. 'I did. I was hoping you'd let me take you to the gala dinner—I realised I'd been taking it for granted that we'd go together, but I haven't asked you formally. Will you let me take you? It will be a good way to celebrate your birthday. I'd like to make it special for you.'

She gazed at him, drinking in the sight of him. 'Thank you, I'd like that, very much.' She studied him thoughtfully, hardly daring to say what was on her mind. 'Actually, I wondered if you might ask Carys.'

'She's going with Ross.'

'Ah.' She looked at him from under her lashes. 'How do you feel about that? Do you mind?'

He seemed puzzled. 'I think it's great—she's perfect for Ross.'

She frowned. 'So it doesn't bother you, her being with him?' She couldn't quite take in his easy answers. She hadn't expected this response at all. How could he be so casual and unconcerned if he'd fallen for Carys?

'Why would it bother me?' He was genuinely mystified by her question, and she finally began to relax a little. Had she misjudged him? 'Am I missing something here?' he said. 'You've been acting oddly ever since Carys went home. Is it because you're missing her?'

'I am,' she admitted. She wasn't ready to tell him the true reason. 'We always get on so well together. I sometimes wish we lived closer to one another.'

He wrapped his arms around her. 'She's only a short flight away—or even a boat ride. I could take you over there whenever you wanted to see her.'

She smiled at him. 'That's really thoughtful of you,' she said softly. 'Thank you for that.' It was typical of him that he should make the offer and she was beginning to feel ashamed of herself for doubting him. Surely there was a logical explanation for his behaviour with Carys? The trouble was, she was too embarrassed to ask him about it.

'You're welcome, any time. I want you to be happy, Alyssa.' He frowned briefly. 'Have you decided what you're going to do about staying on in the Bahamas? I hate the thought of you going away. If it's work that worries you, I know there's room for another doctor in the emergency department at the hospital here. There would be no problem getting you in there.'

'Do you think so?'

'I know it,' he said firmly. 'Everyone talks about how much you did for the patients who ended up in the hospital, and because of you they're all recovering. You know about the car-crash victims, they're both doing well. And Alex has been discharged and is walking again with just a stick to help him—sooner or later he'll be able to cope without that.'

'Yes, I saw him the other day. He came on to the film set to say hello to everyone.'

'You see what I'm saying? He's doing fine. And so is Lewis, now that they've found the right antibiotic. Admittedly, it was touch and go for a while, but now he's getting better every day.'

'It just goes to show what a marvellous hospital system you have here.'

He hugged her to him. 'Seriously, Alyssa...it gave me hope when you said you would go on with your work as a doctor. It would have been such a waste if you'd let it all go. But you could just as easily do that work here, couldn't you? You don't need to go back to the UK, do you?'

'I suppose I could stay...but what is there for me here? Why would you want me to stay? You've never wanted to get deeply involved with anyone before this, have you?'

'Things are different now.' His hand smoothed over the length of her spine. 'I dread the thought of you going away. I want you to stay here, with me. Ever since the accident last week, since I saw Ross's car there and thought you were involved in the crash, I've been churned up inside, imagining what it would be like if you weren't around. It was the same when I saw the tree through Ross's windscreen and thought you might be hurt—I couldn't understand why I cared so much. I'd never felt that way about any woman before.'

She lifted a hand to his cheek, scarcely able to believe what he was saying. 'Do you mean it?'

'Of course I do.' He wrapped her fingers in his and kissed the palm of her hand. 'You can't imagine what it was like for me, thinking that you might be injured. It struck me like a blow to the stomach that I couldn't bear it if you weren't with me.'

Her heart leapt. 'I didn't think it was possible for you to feel that way.'

'Believe it.' It was a heartfelt admission, and she felt his body shudder next to hers. 'And then when you said you were going away, it was like a double blow.' He frowned. 'Alyssa, I know your parents miss you and you miss them—but they could come and visit any time, couldn't they? There's plenty of room for them to stay at the house.'

'You wouldn't mind that…them coming over to stay in the apartment? I mean, it was different with Carys, because you already knew her.'

'Of course I wouldn't mind.' He kissed her tenderly on the lips. 'I want you to stay on and think of the apartment as your own—' He broke off, suddenly intent, searching her face for her response. 'In fact, I'd sooner turn it back into a house and do away with the two apartments.'

'I don't understand,' she said, suddenly confused. 'Are you saying you want me to live with you?'

'Yes, that's exactly what I'm saying.' He ran his hands over her arms, thrilling her with his gentle caresses. 'I want to keep you close, Alyssa. When you told me you were thinking of leaving it made me realise how badly I needed you to stay.' His fingers trailed lightly over her cheek. 'I can't bear to lose you, Alyssa. Will you stay here and marry me so that we can be together for always?'

She pulled in a sharp breath. She wanted to believe that he meant what he said, but her head was reeling from the sudden shock of his proposal. 'But you—you said you didn't believe in commitment… You've never wanted to settle down with any woman.'

'Because I'd never met the right woman until now.' His arms circled her once more and he kissed her, a long, thorough, fervent kiss that left her breathless and sent sweet ripples of ecstasy to flow throughout her body.

'I just know we'll be perfect together,' he said, coming up for air, his voice rough around the edges. 'It won't be like it was for my parents— I'm not the same person as my father. I don't need to go looking at other women because I know you're the one for me. I love you. I thought—' He broke off. 'It felt as though you loved me, too.' He looked at her, his eyes shimmering with passionate intensity.

She smiled, her lips parting in invitation. 'I do,

Connor. I do. I wasn't sure you could love me in return.'

'What's not to love? You're gentle, thoughtful, caring…I've never met anyone like you, and I know we make up two halves of the whole. We're right for one another. I just needed to get my head right and see past the mistakes my father made, that's all. That's not going to happen with us. I know that we're right for one another.'

'That's how I feel, too.' She wrapped her arms around him and he gave a deep sigh of contentment, holding her close for a long time while the birds called to one another overhead and the sea lapped desultorily at the fringes of the beach.

After a while, he stirred and said huskily, 'I'd almost forgotten your birthday present. It's in a drawer in the apartment.' He clasped her hand firmly in his. 'Come with me and I'll get it for you.'

They walked back along the beach towards the house. 'I wasn't sure what to do for the best, but then I talked to Carys, and she said what I had in mind would be just right.' He frowned. 'I hope you like it. I'm still not sure… I mean, I could have…' He stopped talking as she came to a halt and placed her fingers on his lips.

'Whatever it is, I know I'll love it, because you gave to me.' She sent him a thoughtful glance. 'Is this what you and Carys were talking about that day—before you took her to the airport?'

He frowned, and she said, 'I saw you both on the deck. Your heads were close together, and at first I thought…well, it doesn't matter what I thought, but perhaps that was when you were discussing it? Is that why you wanted to drive her there?'

He nodded, but studied her cautiously. 'What went through your mind when you saw us?'

She wriggled her shoulders. 'Nothing. It isn't important.'

He curled his fingers around her upper arms in a firm but gentle clasp. 'You thought I was making a play for her, didn't you?'

She tried to escape from his grasp but he wasn't letting her go until she answered him.

'Okay, yes… It did cross my mind. Only I gave

it a lot of thought and decided I had to learn to trust you. If I couldn't do that, we were doomed, and I really wanted us to have a chance.'

He gave a shuddery sigh. 'Next time you have any doubts or worries, talk to me about them. Promise me?'

'I will. I promise.' She gave him a tremulous smile. 'It was hard for me, Connor. I was badly hurt when James cheated on me, and I could see the same thing happening all over again.' She breathed deeply. 'Then I came to my senses and decided that I was willing to risk everything by putting my faith in you.'

'I will never, ever let you down, Alyssa. Believe me.'

He tugged on her hand and they started towards the house once more. 'Mind you,' he said, almost as an afterthought, 'I had to explain my motives to Ross when I arrived back home. He wasn't at all happy that I'd pipped him to the post by driving Carys to the airport.'

Alyssa laughed. 'Yes, I remember he was very quiet that night.'

They went into Connor's apartment and he went straight over to a bureau in the sitting room and took out a box that was about half the size of a shoebox. He held it out to her.

'Happy birthday,' he said.

She took it from him, gazing at it in wonder. It was beautifully wrapped in gold foil and tied with a pretty silver ribbon. 'It's so lovely, it seems a shame to open it,' she said softly.

'Please do. I really need to know if you like it, if I've done the right thing…I could always…'

She stopped him with a glance and a slight rise of her eyebrow. He laughed. 'Okay, I won't say any more. I've never felt so nervous…'

Carefully, she undid the wrapping and there inside was an exquisite, hand-carved jewellery box, heart-shaped and decorated with an inlaid pattern and delicate enamelling in the shape of a rose.

'Oh, Connor,' she gasped. 'This is beautiful. You made it yourself, didn't you? That's why you were anxious. You shouldn't have been. It's absolutely lovely.'

He breathed a sigh of relief. 'Open it up,' he urged her.

She did as he asked, lifting the lid to reveal a velvet lined interior with sections for necklaces and rings. And in the centre there was another small box, again with an enamelled flower decoration. She lifted it out, and Connor took the jewellery box from her, putting it to one side on a table.

Alyssa's heart began to pound. 'Is this what I think it is?'

He nodded but didn't say anything more, and she carefully opened the box.

Nestling on a bed of silk was a sparkling diamond ring. The gemstones were dazzling, reflecting the sunlight, and the flawless setting took her breath away.

'I've never seen anything so lovely,' she said huskily. 'It's stunning...'

'That's another reason I had to have Carys's help,' he murmured. 'I needed to get the right size, and she said she had a ring that fitted you. We took the measurement from it.'

'No wonder you were so secretive,' she breathed. 'I'd no idea.'

'Let me slip it on your finger,' he said. He smiled. 'Third finger, left hand…' He held up the ring and pulled in a deep breath. 'Will you marry me, Alyssa?'

'Oh, yes. I will. I do love you, Connor,' she said, her voice husky with emotion.

'I love you.'

He slipped the ring on her finger, and they stood by the open doors of his sitting room, arms around one another, gazing at the ring and looking out over the vista of the ocean. Alyssa sighed happily. This was truly their paradise island, and a dream come true.

* * * * *